LINDA LAEL MILLER

CHRISTMAS IN PAINTED PONY CREEK

CANARY STREET PRESS

CANARY
STREET
PRESS™

Recycling programs
for this product may
not exist in your area.

ISBN-13: 978-1-335-43067-0

Christmas in Painted Pony Creek

Canary Street Press
22 Adelaide St. West, 41st Floor
Toronto, Ontario M5H 4E3, Canada
CanaryStPress.com

Printed in U.S.A.

For my kid sister Pam, fighting the good fight.
You're stronger than you can ever imagine, and I'm so proud of you.

❄ 1 ❄

Late August
Five miles outside Painted Pony Creek, Montana

Red and blue lights splashed against the rear window of the old car, blurred by sheets of rain.

"Mommy," chirped five-year-old Isabel from her booster chair in the back seat, "are we arrested?"

Tessa Stafford sighed, smiling moistly, and lifted her forehead from the steering wheel. She turned her head to look back at her daughter. "No, sweetheart," she replied. "We haven't done anything wrong."

Isabel, a precocious blonde child with bright blue eyes, peered through the steam-fogged windows. "Then why is there a police person out there?"

Tessa widened her smile—it was an effort—and hoped her eyes didn't look as puffy and red as they felt. Not only was the car out of gas, but one of the front tires was flat. "I'm sure they've stopped to help," she answered. "Everything's okay, buttercup."

Was it, though? While she and Isabel certainly weren't on the run from the law, it was possible that her ex's stepmother had managed to trump up some kind of bogus charge against Tessa. A narcissistic demon of a woman, she wanted custody of Isabel—her only grandchild—and was willing to go to considerable lengths to win.

Although no less than three judges had ruled against her in family court, Marjory Laughlin was undaunted. She was wealthy, with plenty of friends in high places, and she considered Tessa unfit to raise a Laughlin.

A rap sounded at the driver's-side window, jolting Tessa out of the worry that was always bubbling away inside her, usually just beneath the surface of her normally calm and quiet personality.

She could just make out a tall woman in a hooded poncho peering in and making a roll-down-the-window gesture.

Tessa obeyed, but a face full of rain almost made her roll it up again.

"Car trouble?" the police officer shouted over the downpour. She was beautiful, with dark skin and full lips.

"Yes!" Tessa yelled in response. "I'm pretty sure one of my front tires is flat, and we're out of gas!" Nothing like having to holler out something you were singularly ashamed of.

The woman nodded, and even though Tessa couldn't exactly read the look in her brown eyes, she gave off a friendly vibe. "You and your little girl okay otherwise? I don't need to send for an ambulance or anything like that?"

Tessa shook her head, then nodded and sighed inwardly, annoyed with herself for the contradiction. "We're fine," she called out.

"No, we're not!" Isabel protested from her perch in back. "It's scary out here, and it's cold, and I need chicken noodle soup!"

The officer leaned closer to the partly open window, laughing, and said, "Well, now, suppose we get you someplace safe and dry and rustle up that soup?"

Now it was Isabel who nodded, vigorously and with resolve.

"My name is Melba Summers," the woman said, raising her voice to be heard as she addressed Isabel. "I'm the chief of police in Painted Pony Creek." She paused, fumbled inside her rain slicker and revealed a gleaming brass badge. "You can trust me." Another pause, then, "Now, I'm going to pull my SUV up as close behind you as I can. Once I've done that, I want you and your mama to jump right out of this car and run like the dickens for my rig. I'll be waiting on the passenger side to help you inside where it's warm, and we'll head on into town and get you fed. How does that sound?"

Isabel pondered a moment, then beamed. "I can run pretty fast," she boasted. "I won a prize last year in preschool."

"In that case," Chief Summers replied with a flash of a smile, "I'd better be quick about this." She shifted her gaze back to Tessa. "I guess I should have asked if this plan suits you," she said.

Tessa, low on money as always, was wondering about the price of the promised soup, among other things.

"The locks don't work," she said, fretting aloud. All her and Isabel's belongings, humble as they were, were stuffed inside this rust bucket of a car. Nothing worth stealing, she supposed, but necessities just the same.

"I'll send somebody to fetch your things, don't you worry about that, and we'll figure out what to do about your car later."

"All right," Tessa finally agreed with a mixture of reluctance and relief.

She, like her daughter, yearned for someplace warm and dry and brightly lit.

Isabel had already unbuckled herself from her booster seat and was pulling on her pink jacket, raising the hood, tugging the drawstrings tight and tying them under her chin.

Tessa smiled. For such a little kid, Isabel was efficient.

Since it was August, Tessa's only coat was packed away in one of the garbage bags jammed into the trunk. She would have to run the rain gauntlet in a sundress and sandals, carrying Isabel in her arms.

Chief Summers hurried back to her SUV, climbed into the driver's seat and pulled the vehicle up to Tessa's rear bumper. Then she honked the horn.

Resigned, Tessa pulled the keys from the ignition, dropped them into her purse and turned, once again, to face Isabel. "Sit tight until I open your door," she said. "I mean it, peanut. Don't make a run for the police car without me, got it?"

A car whizzed by, tires spraying water high into the air. The danger was all too obvious, and Isabel was, after all, only five years old.

Tessa took a deep breath and sprang out of the car,

gasping as rain spattered in her face. Then, holding her breath, she checked as best she could, given the low visibility, for the chief's vehicle.

The woman was waiting. Tessa opened Isabel's door, gathered the little girl in her arms and ran. The chief flung open the front passenger door of her rig when Tessa and Isabel reached her, and half boosted, half shoved them inside.

Soon, Chief Summers was behind the wheel, ebony face shining with rainwater and triumph. "Buckle up," she ordered cheerfully.

"Don't you have a car seat?" Isabel asked. Tessa was very strict when it came to car seats.

"Not today," answered the chief. "Just this once, we'll go without."

With that, the chief checked all her mirrors, and then she blasted her siren once, just in case. Her lights were still flashing, and she backed up a little, pulled out onto the highway and left Tessa's abandoned car rocking a little from the force of her passing.

"Let's see about that soup," she said.

Less than ten minutes later, they were pulling up to a restaurant with a neon sign perched on the roof that read Bailey's.

The rain hadn't let up, so the three of them got out of the SUV and made a dash for the entrance.

Inside, lights gleamed, pushing back the darkness of the summer storm along with some of Tessa's misgivings.

A tall blonde woman of a certain age, blessed with the finest bone structure Tessa had ever seen, welcomed them warmly. According to the tag on her uniform shirt, her name was Alice.

"Good heavens," she spouted. "You're all drenched to the skin!" She turned to one of the waitstaff, a pretty young girl, and said, "Carly, run upstairs and get some towels, will you please?"

Carly hastened away.

Melba Summers took off her slicker and hung it on one of the hooks alongside the entrance, careful to keep it away from the light sweaters and windbreakers already there.

"This is—" The chief paused, frowned. "I guess I didn't get around to asking your names," she admitted.

"I'm Tessa Stafford and this is my daughter—"

"Isabel!" the little girl interjected with proud enthusiasm.

Carly returned with towels, and once the three wayfarers had been ruffled to a semblance of dryness, Alice led them to a table by the jukebox.

"Coffee? Tea?" she asked once they were settled.

"Do you have chicken noodle soup?" Isabel wanted to know. "I like the kind that comes in a red-and-white can."

Mentally, Tessa counted the money in her tattered wallet, tucked away in her equally tattered purse. She wasn't *quite* broke—she'd set aside enough cash, after leaving her last job back in South Dakota, for a week or two in a cheap motel room, a dozen packets of ramen noodles and a jug of milk—but she had to be very careful.

She and Isabel had wound up staying in shelters more than once when funds ran low, and they'd stood in their share of soup lines, too. While Tessa had been profoundly grateful for the help, she'd felt ashamed of needing to accept charity. She'd never been able to shake the feeling that other people needed food and a bed more than she did.

In point of fact, she would gladly have gone hungry and slept in the car, no matter the weather, to keep Isabel safe.

"Chicken noodle soup coming right up, young lady," Alice told Isabel. "How about a glass of milk, too?"

"Yes, please," Isabel replied.

"Coffee for me," said Melba Summers.

Alice gave Tessa a questioning glance.

"Coffee sounds wonderful," she said uncertainly, and with a wavering smile. Her sundress was soaked, and she was keeping her arms crossed in case her bra showed through.

"On the house," Alice said gently, and headed for the kitchen.

It was as Tessa let her gaze follow the older woman that the man at the counter caught her eye.

He'd turned on the swiveling stool to watch the scene unfold, evidently.

Somewhere in his thirties, Tessa guessed, tall and damp from the storm, he wore old jeans, scuffed boots and a lightweight flannel shirt over a T-shirt that had seen its best days long ago. His hair was a butternut color, thick and ever so slightly too long.

His eyes were blue—almost turquoise—and a light stubble bristled on his jaw.

An unaccountable jolt went through Tessa the moment their gazes met, and she felt a flush rise to her cheeks, burning there.

Definitely visible.

Blood thumped in Tessa's ears, pushing back sound, muffling it, as though she were under water.

WTH? she thought.

It was Chief Summers who broke the strange silence. "Jesse McKettrick," she said with a broad grin. "Just the man I wanted to see. You driving that big old show-off truck of yours today? The one with a winch?"

Jesse left the stool to amble toward them, moving with a slight and probably unconscious swagger. His grin struck Tessa with an impact, like a gust of warm, hard wind.

"Yes, Chief," he said. "The truck's right outside."

His eyes rested on Tessa as he spoke, and she saw amused curiosity dancing in them.

Lord have mercy, he was about the handsomest man she had ever seen, dressed in work clothes, and he had an air of easy confidence about him.

Tessa resisted an urge to glance at his left-hand ring finger. A man like this would be married, or at least have a girlfriend.

And even if by some miracle he was single, she concluded grimly, he wouldn't be interested in a virtual nomad like her.

"Good," the chief was saying when Tessa came back

to herself. "Because we've got a car that needs to be towed to town."

Jesse gave another one of those slow, lethal grins. "Well, Chief," he drawled, still looking at Tessa, "if you're not going to make the introductions, I will." He put out a hand. "My name, as you heard, is Jesse McKettrick. I didn't catch yours."

A woman could tumble right into those blue-green eyes, head over heels and helpless to break the fall.

"Tessa Stafford," she replied gruffly, and wished she'd cleared her throat before speaking.

Which would have been even more embarrassing.

"And I'm Isabel," her daughter announced with her usual aplomb.

The man bowed a little. "Honored to meet you, Isabel," he replied solemnly.

Isabel beamed. "I'm five," she said, "and I can already read. Mom taught me *ages* ago."

Jesse looked suitably impressed. "You'll probably skip first grade entirely when you start school," he said, speculating. "Maybe second and third, too."

Isabel turned serious, slowly shaking her head from side to side. "Mom won't let me skip kindergarten, even. She says there's no hurry, and I need to be with kids my own age. So that's where I'm going next—

kindergarten." The child stopped, frowned thought-fully. "*If* we stop driving in some town where there's a school. We drive *a lot*."

Tessa closed her eyes for a moment. Sighed.

Isabel had a tendency to overshare, obviously.

Before anyone could offer a reply to the most recent news flash, Carly arrived with a tray holding a steaming bowl of soup, a packet of crackers, a glass of milk and two coffees.

Jesse stepped aside to give the girl room to pass, but he didn't walk away.

Tessa wished he would.

Hoped he wouldn't.

Being near him stirred a subtle, daring kind of joy in her, and that was unsettling.

She wasn't staying here in—what was the name again? Something Creek?—because she hadn't put enough space between herself and Isabel and Marjory Ducking Laughlin.

She would work awhile—assuming she could find a job—get the car fixed and hit the road again.

When she found a place that was safe for her and her child, she would know it. Then they would settle down, hopefully for good, and make a life for themselves. At long last.

Isabel's eyes widened with pleasure as she admired the bowl of chicken noodle soup in front of her. With great delicacy, she picked up her spoon, dipped it into the broth and blew on it.

She always saved the noodles for last.

Watching her, Tessa felt a pang of desperate love for her baby, her girl. She was growing up so fast.

She blinked back tears, looked up and realized both the chief and Jesse were watching her. Again, her cheeks burned.

"Where do you want me to haul this car to, Melba?" he asked. Despite his smooth manner, he seemed a little off his game, just in that moment.

Instead of answering, Melba turned to Tessa with a question of her own. "Do you have someplace to stay? Maybe with family or friends?"

Tessa shook her head. "No friends or family." Her stomach growled audibly, and she hoped no one else had heard, including Isabel, who would surely comment. "I guess if there's an inexpensive motel nearby—"

She hadn't noticed Alice clearing a neighboring table. "There's an empty apartment right upstairs," she said. "Carly used to live there, but she moved back in with her parents last week. She's headed off to college in a

few days." There was a pause. "Do you have any experience waiting tables, Tessa?"

Melba grinned, saying nothing, and took a sip of
coffee.

Tessa, stunned by this apparent good luck—a rarity,
in her experience—stared at Alice, afraid she'd heard
wrong.

Things like this didn't happen to her.

"I've worked in a few restaurants and diners," she
managed to say.

"Good," Alice said, as though the whole thing had
been decided. In the next moment, she was giving the
girl, Carly, instructions—make sure there were clean
sheets and towels upstairs, then stock the fridge with a
few staples from the restaurant's kitchen.

"Jesse, you go and get Tessa's car," Melba put in.

Alice spoke up again. "You can leave it in back for
now. Carly and I will help carry in Tessa's belongings,
along with Isabel's, of course, and get them settled."

"What about references?" Tessa asked. "And we need
to discuss the rent—"

"We'll cover all that later," Alice said dismissively.
"You just relax and I'll get you something to eat."

Tessa opened her mouth, closed it again.

Was this really happening?

Indeed, it was.

Without another word, Jesse went to the row of hooks beside the front door, shrugged into a faded denim jacket, flipped up the collar and donned his cowboy hat. He left without looking back, and that was a good thing, as far as Tessa was concerned, because if he had, he'd have caught her staring at him.

Alice had gone into the kitchen.

Chief Summers finished her coffee, sighed and said, "I'd better get back to work. My department is short-staffed at the moment." She studied Tessa with kindly concern. "Are you sure you're okay?" she asked quietly. "If you need—" she glanced at Isabel, who was enjoying her soup "—well, *protection*, I can ask Sheriff Garrett to send over a deputy."

Struck by this woman's perception, not to mention her kindness, Tessa shook her head quickly. She was appreciative, but she was also exhausted and overwhelmed, and, besides, she'd taken up enough of this woman's time and energy for one night.

Maybe, at some point, she would confide in Chief Summers, but not tonight.

"We'll be fine," she said, hoping that was true.

Marjory Laughlin was pure hell-spawn and she probably wasn't above sending goons to carry out her delusional wishes—once, she'd nearly succeeded in kidnapping the little girl, showing up at day care and playing the role of loving grandmother. Isabel had protested, fighting her way out of Marjory's grasp and screaming, "Stranger! Stranger!"

As she'd been taught to do.

Publicly shamed, Marjory had backed off.

At least for a little while.

Yes, they were still in danger, but, for tonight anyway, Tessa decided, she could let down her guard a little. She and Isabel were safe for the moment.

And they didn't have to stay in a cheap roadside motel, like they usually did.

Tessa sighed inwardly and offered up a silent prayer of gratitude.

Aloud, she said, "Thank you so much, Chief Summers. For everything." Tears burned behind Tessa's eyes, threatened to overflow.

The chief patted Tessa's hand sympathetically and produced a business card and pen from the breast pocket of her uniform shirt, then scrawled ten digits onto the back. "This is my private cell number. Don't hesitate to call if you need some help, night or day."

Tessa nodded, bit her lower lip. One word and she'd dissolve into a torrent of emotion.

"And my name isn't 'Chief.' It's Melba."

Again, Tessa merely nodded. She was tired, chilled and hungry, and humbled by the generosity of this woman.

Just then, Alice reappeared, carrying a second bowl of steaming soup. She set it down in front of Tessa as Melba went to the door and donned her rain poncho, which was still dripping.

"Come back when you can stay longer," Alice called. "I want to hear how Dan and the kids are doing."

Melba smiled. "Tomorrow's my day off," she responded, opening the door as she spoke. "Maybe we'll all stop in for supper and a catch-up."

The exchange gave Tessa a pang in the region of her heart. What would it be like to have friends, to be part of a community?

Silently, she pulled herself together. She knew she was teetering on the edge of an abyss of despair and self-pity, and she couldn't afford to fall in. She had to be strong for Isabel.

She had to keep it together, no matter what, because if she didn't, Marjory might find out—she had her ways—and then swoop in and demand custody of Isabel. Again.

Tessa shuddered.

"Cold?" Alice Bailey asked quietly, as the door closed behind Melba Summers.

Tessa shook her head. "No." She breathed in the savory steam rising from her soup, a mixture of black beans, lentils and various vegetables. The aroma was nourishing, all by itself. "Thank you, Mrs. Bailey," she murmured, looking away again and blinking rapidly.

"It's Alice," came the brisk response, "and you're welcome. If the soup doesn't fill you up, I'll throw together a sandwich."

Isabel, quiet all this time, finally spoke up. "Is everybody around here as nice as you and the police lady?" she asked.

Alice pondered the question, then said, "Pretty much. We like to look out for each other here in Painted Pony Creek."

Isabel nodded. Sometimes, she seemed far more grown up than she was, and that saddened Tessa. Not for the first time, she longed fiercely to give her daughter a normal, secure life. Send her to the same school for more than a few months at a time, provide a real home, however humble, and maybe even someday a stepfather. Brothers and sisters.

"That's a pretty name for a town," Isabel remarked.

Then she frowned thoughtfully. "Is there a real painted pony?"

Alice smiled warmly and glanced at Tessa. "There was, a long time ago," the older woman answered. "These days, we don't decorate our horses—except maybe for parades."

"Oh," Isabel said, apparently satisfied.

Then she yawned. "Can we sleep now, Mommy?" she asked.

Tessa leaned over, kissed her child on the top of her head. "Soon, baby. Just let me finish this delicious soup."

Jesse found the car alongside the road that led to the neighboring community of Silver Hills.

The ancient rig looked like it was held together by spit, duct tape and a prayer. He backed up to within a yard or two of its front bumper.

The rain was still coming down by the bucketload, but he didn't want to mess around with his rain gear. So he braced himself, shoved open the door of his truck and jumped out. His booted feet landed square in a muddy puddle, and the resulting splash sloshed against his jeans. Merely damp before, they were soaked to his knees now.

He sighed and moved between the two vehicles, bending to squint at the dented license plate.

Massachusetts.

Tessa Stafford and her little daughter were a long, long way from home.

And unless his practiced intuition was putting out false signals, they were running from something—or someone.

While he cranked the winch and attached it to the front of the old car, he speculated, trying to ignore the rain trickling down his back from the collar of his jacket.

Who or what was Tessa trying to get away from?

Although she'd tried valiantly to hide it, he knew she was afraid, for herself and for her kid.

So who was after them? An abusive husband, maybe? Or a bad boyfriend?

Possibly, Tessa had been a battered woman.

The idea of some crap-stain pecker-head of a human being manhandling Tessa and her child, or *any* woman or child, galled Jesse McKettrick in a way few things did.

Mostly, he was a sensible, even-tempered guy.

He'd been raised, after all, by caring, competent adults. Taught to respect women as equals.

He was well educated—an attorney, in fact, licensed in California and Montana, though he hadn't practiced in a while.

He was also peacefully divorced, with no kids.

He secured the winch and tested it with a hard yank, which also served to disperse some of the adrenaline his speculations about Tessa's situation had generated.

What the hell did he know?

Tessa was a stranger to him, albeit a very intriguing one, and he knew nothing about her or her past.

Even if somebody *was* on her trail, it was no business of his.

Hell, maybe *she* was the guilty one, a beautiful young con woman trying to leave her latest victim in the dust, looking for her next mark and not above using her own child to rack up sympathy points.

If so, she was off to a good start. She'd turned Melba and Alice—both smart women—into her champions right out of the chute.

Jesse climbed back into the truck, feeling chilled and longing for a hot shower. And calling himself out for thinking the worst of the mysterious Ms. Stafford, with her scrap-metal car and her cute kid.

He shifted the truck into low gear and pulled forward.

The tow chain drew taut with a muffled *clank*, and

he tossed aside his hat, shoved one hand through his wet hair in sheer frustration.

He needed to get some perspective.

And that, he decided glumly, was going to take some time.

❄ 2 ❄

Early November

Down with the giant inflatable black cat gracing the roof of the hardware store, up with the equally enormous plastic turkey.

So long Halloween, hello Thanksgiving, Tessa thought from where she sat in Bailey's restaurant and bar, smiling over the rim of her coffee cup as she watched from the front window. Her shift—breakfast and lunch this week—had just ended, and her feet hurt, but her heart was light.

Her life had changed a lot in the three months since she and Isabel had arrived in Painted Pony Creek, all for the better.

So far.

She hadn't heard from Isabel's bio-dad, Brent, or his harpy of a stepmother in all that time, but that didn't mean she could stop being on the lookout.

Brent wasn't much of a threat; he was probably too busy partying, womanizing and spending the family fortune to give his accidental daughter a thought. In fact, he'd been so horrified when Tessa had tracked him down to tell him she was pregnant with his child that he'd literally backpedaled, all color draining from his handsome, expensively tanned face.

At the time, he'd been interning at his grandfather's successful marketing firm, while Tessa was barely holding on to her two part-time jobs. She rented a shabby room in a shabby boardinghouse, rode the bus to and from work and tried to squeeze in a few online classes, which she could barely afford.

"If you're expecting me to propose—" a flustered Brent had begun, there in the lobby of the family skyscraper, which stood in the heart of Boston.

Tessa had interrupted with a contemptuous shake of her head and a terse, "No. You're the *last* person I'd want to marry, Brent Laughlin."

His Adam's apple bobbed as he swallowed, fumbled through his suit pockets and pulled out his wallet. "You can have the pregnancy terminated. I'll pay for everything."

He opened the wallet and held out a sheaf of hundred-dollar bills.

Tessa made no move to accept his offering. "That won't be happening, either," she replied.

"You're *keeping* the baby?"

"Yes."

"Why?"

It was telling, she thought, that he didn't *know* why.

Telling, but not surprising, considering how selfish and entitled this golden boy could be.

Not that she'd realized that when they were dating. Back then, she'd been besotted beyond all common sense.

He, on the other hand, had simply been slumming.

"'Why?' That's an insipid question," Tessa remarked, "even for you."

"Come on, Tessa," came Brent's hoarse, angry protest. He was flushed and kept looking around the lobby, probably worried that she'd make a scene. "This isn't 1950. Women terminate pregnancies all the time!"

"What other women choose to do with their own bodies is their business, not mine. I *want* this baby."

"That's crazy," Brent snapped, practically baring his

teeth at her by then. "You're a *waitress*. How are you planning to support a child? If you think I'm going to help, you're sadly mistaken."

"I can manage on my own," she responded. "Except for one thing."

He glared at her. "Such as?" he growled.

"Such as a college fund for *your* child."

"You don't think I'm really going to agree to that, do you? For all I know, you're carrying some other guy's kid, not mine. This is a scam!"

Tessa stood her ground. "We'll have a paternity test done as soon as the baby's born, unless it's possible to have it done sooner—I'd have to ask my doctor about that. If the results prove you're the baby daddy, you'll set up a fund, pronto. You don't have to give me access to it, in case you're wondering, but when our child turns eighteen, the funds will be available to her. Do we have a deal?"

He bristled, red from the neck up. Clenched his hands into fists, though wisely he refrained from raising them to her. "Suppose I say no? This whole thing is pretty suspicious, if you ask me. We weren't together that long!"

"Long enough to conceive a baby," Tessa reminded him.

They'd parted ways after a mere three months, when

Tessa had accidentally learned that Brent was not only a vain, spoiled polo prince, he was also a cheater. She was pregnant at the time, of course, but she hadn't realized it yet; her cycles had always been irregular and, besides, she was dealing with a broken heart.

She'd fallen fast and hard for Brent Laughlin, and he'd crushed her.

"You're trying to rip me off!" he accused. "So, no, Tessa. N.O. You're going to have to find yourself another gravy train to ride, because this one has left the station!"

Tessa arched an eyebrow, cool on the outside, panicked and furious on the inside. "You might want to rethink that decision," she said mildly.

"Why should I?" he demanded, still angry, but smug now, too. A smirk tugged at one corner of his mouth. The mouth she'd once loved to kiss.

"If you don't, I'll be forced to—" here, she widened her eyes "—*tell your mommy.*"

"That's blackmail!"

"No, Brent, it's simple expediency. I'm not asking for marriage, or medical expenses, or even child support. I can take care of my—*our*—baby on my own. But she deserves to go to college when the time comes, and I mean to make sure she isn't denied an education."

"She?" Brent repeated. "You couldn't even muster up a boy? I might have been amenable to terms if you weren't expecting a girl."

Never, in all her life, had Tessa wanted to sucker punch someone as badly as she did in that moment.

With great effort, she restrained herself.

This encounter was all about her daughter's future, and she wasn't about to blow that by landing herself in the hoosegow on an assault charge.

"And *you* reminded *me* that this isn't 1950," she answered coolly. Calmly. "Women need an education as much as men, you arrogant shit."

Brent had thrown back his head and laughed then, though there was no humor in the sound. He must have forgotten the need to preserve his A-list family's reputation, because the sound was loud and people were starting to stare.

Mike and Dave, a pair of burly bouncers at the club where Tessa tended bar on weekends, stopped pretending to study their phone screens and took a few steps toward her and Brent. She'd brought them along in case Brent got physical.

He'd never done that before, but then, she'd never had to tell him he was about to become a father.

Given the pulsing vein in his forehead and the way

he kept clenching his fists, she was glad she'd taken precautions.

"I guess you'd know about wanting an education," Brent taunted, leaning in so close that Tessa felt the heat of his breath on her face. "Since you don't have one."

He'd definitely struck a nerve, but Tessa tried hard not to let it show.

Sensing that he'd gotten to her, Brent chuckled cruelly and whispered, "But wait. You *do* have a GED, don't you? I guess I spoke too soon."

Mike and Dave must have picked up on the rising bad vibes, because they came closer, approaching from opposite sides of the lobby.

So much for subtlety.

They clearly wanted to bounce Brent back and forth between them like a medicine ball at the gym.

Tessa stopped them with a look.

She straightened her back and lifted her chin, stared directly and unflinchingly into Brent's blue eyes. "I don't really care what you think of me, Brent," she said evenly, "since my opinion of you is lower still." She drew a deep breath, let it out slowly. When she was alone, she'd have the luxury of crying, letting out the tangle of anger and frustration and fear inside her, but it was out of the question in the moment.

She didn't dare show the slightest weakness.

Surprisingly, Brent relented a little, took a less threatening stance. Maybe he spotted Tessa's volunteer bodyguards.

"Listen," he said more evenly, though he was still shoving words through his teeth. "I guess you've got a point. We'll do the DNA test. If, by some wild turn of events, you really are carrying my baby, we'll discuss a trust fund with my lawyer."

"I'm not going to let this go," Tessa warned, suspicious of his convenient acquiescence.

He laughed again, without amusement. "Whatever," he said, and he turned and walked away.

As soon as the elevator doors closed behind him, Tessa's knees buckled.

If it hadn't been for Dave and Mike, rushing in to grip her by the elbows, she would have collapsed into a heap in the fancy, marble-floored lobby of Laughlin Enterprises, International.

Tessa was jolted back to the present when the little bell over the restaurant door jingled merrily.

Jesse McKettrick stepped over the threshold, looking way too good in a sawdust-covered vintage band T-shirt—the Grateful Dead—a denim jacket, scruffy boots and old jeans.

The place was empty, except for the corner table, where eight middle-aged book club members sat— seven women and Charlie, Tessa's favorite, who sported an English tweed waistcoat, woolen trousers, a pristine white shirt and an ascot.

The man was kindness personified.

"Hey," Jesse said to Tessa, after acknowledging the twittered greetings from the elderly members of the book club with a nod and a smile. "Is there any apple pie left?"

Tessa laughed, relieved to be distracted from both her memories of the long-ago confrontation with Brent and the huge plastic turkey now dancing in the breeze above the hardware store.

"One piece, I think. Have a seat and I'll grab it for you." She paused, feeling a blush play over her cheekbones. She and Jesse were nothing more than acquaintances, but seeing him always made her feel as if she'd swallowed a tiny, anxious bird, frantic to fly away. "Do you want ice cream with it? And coffee?"

"Both, please," Jesse said, ambling over to the counter and settling onto a stool. She loved the way he walked with a slight swagger and an air of quiet confidence. "Vanilla for the ice cream, black for the coffee."

"Got it," Tessa said lightly. Technically, she was off

duty for the day, and her coworker Miranda was in the kitchen, tying on her apron, ready to start the second shift, but one more customer wasn't going to be a problem.

Especially not *this* customer.

While she was dishing up the last piece of apple pie, along with a generous scoop of vanilla ice cream, Miranda came over and nudged her lightly in the ribs. She was about the same age as Alice Bailey; the two women had been fast friends for years.

"That man," Miranda whispered pointedly, "is trying to work up the nerve to ask you out. Why not flirt a little? Make it easier for him?"

"You and your imagination," Tessa whispered back good-naturedly. "Jesse McKettrick is *way* out of my league, in case you haven't noticed. He's just being nice."

Miranda's happy, expectant expression slipped. She kept her voice low, but the counter wasn't far from the kitchen and the thought of Jesse overhearing such a conversation was too embarrassing for words. "'Out of your league'? Look in the mirror, woman. You happen to be beautiful."

"Stop it," Tessa all but hissed, picking up the plate

of pie and ice cream and heading for the door leading to the dining area.

Jesse was scrolling casually on his phone when Tessa set his food in front of him, along with a fork and spoon. It was only when she'd turned to the coffee machine to fill a mug for him that he spoke.

"Miranda's right," he said quietly. "You're beautiful. And I *have* been working up my courage to ask you out."

Tessa was mortified, even as a wild, reckless thrill surged through her. For a long moment, she just stood there, coffee mug in hand, unable to turn around and face him.

Jesse had always been kind to her, from that first rainy night when he'd collected her car from the roadside and brought it back to town. And, yes, over the three months following, she'd caught herself daydreaming about him many times. All the same, Brent had taught her a bitter, lasting lesson.

Right or wrong, there *was* a wide gap between the haves and have-nots.

And at present, that gap was all too obvious.

Jesse had a law degree. She had a GED and a few random college courses under her belt. Jesse came from an established, loving family. She was the daughter of a troubled woman who had abandoned her to the foster-care system when she was only eight years old. She'd never known who her father was.

Jesse could afford to do random legal work, mostly pro bono, while indulging in his hobby, carpentry. He was in the process of building the main street of an Old West town, complete with saloon, marshal's office and general store. The place wouldn't be open to visitors until midsummer, but people were already traveling to Painted Pony Creek from all over the region to try to sneak a peek at the attraction.

She, by contrast, worked in food service and, even with all the kindnesses the Baileys had extended to her, was earning minimum wage and reasonably good tips. And it took all of that to provide for herself and Isabel and put aside something for emergencies.

Tessa was well versed in emergencies.

She and Isabel had stayed in the Baileys' apartment above the restaurant for their first month in town. But the place was fancy, at least from her viewpoint, and despite their objections, she'd known she was taking advantage of people who had already given her so much.

Now she and her daughter lived in a modest little rental house within walking distance of Bailey's and two blocks from the church complex where Isabel attended kindergarten and day care.

Tessa wasn't stupid; she knew her view of things had been messed up by her childhood, by the hard years after she'd aged out of the system, and, of course, the whole Brent experience. She probably needed therapy—forget the "probably"—but that, like so many other things, was out of her financial reach.

"If I can't get an answer," Jesse said when she half turned from the coffee machine, "maybe you could look at me?"

Tessa looked.

Before she could speak, Isabel came bursting through the door to the kitchen, waving a paper.

"We made turkeys!" the little girl cried, full of the joy of accomplishment. "Look, Mommy! We used our hands!"

On days when she worked, she or Miranda met Isabel at the church and brought her back to Bailey's for lunch. After day care, Ms. Atwater, one of the childminders, accompanied Isabel as far as the restaurant, claiming it was on her way home anyway. Julia Atwater was one of the many people who made Painted Pony Creek such a special place.

Isabel thrust the paper under Tessa's nose. "See? Our

fingers made the tail, and the wings, and the head and the neck are from my thumb!"

"That's wonderful," Tessa said, admiring the standard kindergarten turkey, neatly and somewhat garishly colored with crayons.

"It looks kind of like that big bird over there!" Isabel said enthusiastically, pointing to the creature atop the hardware store. "Teacher says the day after Thanksgiving the volunteer fire department will put up a Santa instead. Plus eight reindeer *and* Rudolph!"

"Wow," Tessa murmured, still off balance from the brief exchange with Jesse.

"*And* there's going to be a Christmas play at the church, too!" Isabel prattled on. "I get to play one of the shepherds watching their flocks by night, and I'm the only one who gets to talk, except for Mary and Joseph and the innkeeper. I'm supposed to point at the ceiling and say, 'Look at all those angels' or something like that."

"Impressive," Tessa said, laughing. God, how she loved this child.

"I'll say," Jesse interjected, from his place at the counter. He wasn't looking at Isabel's paper, though. He was watching Tessa's face.

Isabel, who, unlike her mother, wasn't the least bit

shy, beamed and hurried around the end of the counter to scramble up onto the stool beside Jesse's. She'd had a lot of practice making the climb, since she spent plenty of time at the restaurant.

Another of the Baileys' kindnesses.

"Would you like to see the turkey I drew?" she asked.

"I sure would," Jesse answered, taking the paper and examining it in great detail. Then he whistled for emphasis. "That's a fine turkey," he said admiringly.

"Even though it's pink and purple?" Isabel inquired. "My very best friend, Eleanor Susan Gwendolyn Gray, says real turkeys aren't pink and purple."

"Eleanor Susan Gwendolyn Gray?" Jesse asked. "Wouldn't it be easier to call your friend Ellie or something like it?"

"Eleanor doesn't do nicknames," Tessa explained, relaxing a little. "With her, it's all or nothing."

It would have been so easy to pretend that this cozy little scenario—herself, Jesse and Isabel gathered into a circle of turkey admiration—was something more than it was.

Like a family, for instance.

Suddenly feeling very tired, Tessa reeled in her scattered emotions. There she went, fantasizing again. "Come on, kiddo," she said cheerfully, pretending Jesse hadn't mentioned thinking she was beautiful and wanting to ask her out just before the onslaught of Isabel. Honestly, the kid's personality was the size of the rooftop turkey. "Let's go home. I have work to do."

It was true. The laundry was piling up and the floors needed to be vacuumed and she hadn't even thought about what she'd make for supper.

"I don't want to go home yet," Isabel objected innocently. "I like it here. It's warm and busy and I don't feel lonesome."

Isabel felt *lonesome*? That was news to Tessa. Her daughter was a happy child, whether alone or with others.

Wasn't she?

Jesse fixed his gaze on Tessa and raised his eyebrows, a slight smile tilting the side of his mouth.

Fortunately, he didn't say anything.

"You're making a town," Isabel said conversationally, turning to look directly up at Jesse. "Like one in a John Wayne movie."

Jesse chuckled. "Yep," he said. "Are you a fan of the Duke?"

"Absolutely," Isabel replied without hesitation. "Mommy says they don't make men like that anymore."

Jesse grinned, giving Tessa a sidelong glance that

doubled the rate of her heartbeat. "Is that right?" he replied, his voice a low, rumbling drawl, full of—well—something she wasn't exactly comfortable identifying.

"Yes," Isabel said, unaware of the subtext.

"Let's go," Tessa repeated, a little tersely this time.

Jesse merely watched her, and she resisted an urge to pull her uniform dress closer to her skin. The man made her feel as though her clothes might fall off, or simply vaporize into nothing.

Isabel sighed heavily and climbed down off the stool, turkey drawing in hand. "Oh, for Pete's sake," she muttered, sounding more like a jaded adult than a little girl.

Jesse looked down at the child, and there was something so patient, so tender, in his expression that Tessa's mixed-up, half-healed heart tripped up again.

"If you and your mom would like a look at Bitter Gulch, let me know. It's definitely the kind of place the Duke would hang out in."

Damn him. Everybody in Painted Pony Creek was curious about the future tourist attraction Jesse was building, and Isabel was no exception.

Nor was Tessa.

"That's coercion," Tessa complained, though without much conviction.

"It's persistence," Jesse replied. "There's a difference."

"What's co-err-shum?" Isabel wanted to know.

"Never mind," said Tessa.

"When?" Isabel asked Jesse. "When can we see Bitter Gulch?"

"Whenever it's convenient for your mom," Jesse said smoothly.

Tessa glared at him. She was tired. Her feet hurt. And she didn't want to get sucked further into her impossible fantasies.

This wasn't a movie on the Hallmark Channel; it was real life.

Spending time with Jesse McKettrick wouldn't help her keep her emotional feet on the ground.

"I'll even throw in supper," Jesse added. "There's a grill in the hotel kitchen, and I'm a halfway decent cook."

Typical lawyer. He wasn't going to quit, obviously.

Isabel was beside her by then, tugging at the sleeve of her blue cardigan sweater. "Please, Mommy? Can we *please* have supper in Bitter Gulch? I'll be the only kid in town who's ever even *been there*."

"True," Jesse mused aloud. "My niece and nephew have visited, but they live in California, so it doesn't count."

Tessa rolled her eyes.

Jesse grinned again.

"Oh, all right," Tessa said, finally conceding, secretly shamed by the eagerness suddenly swelling within her, crowding her organs into a tight bunch. "When?"

"How about tonight?" Jesse asked. "I can pick you up in a few hours. You're living in the old Farriday house, right?"

Feeling both defeated and triumphant, Tessa simply nodded.

"Six o'clock?" he added.

"Okay," Tessa said with a glance at the clock on the wall behind her.

Three hours. She had three hours to get ready.

Three *years* wouldn't have been enough.

"It will be dark at six o'clock," Isabel said fretfully. "How can we see anything in the dark?"

"Unlike most Old West towns, the Gulch is wired for electricity. And there are streetlights," Jesse explained, standing up and tossing some cash onto the counter. "Besides, the moon is almost full."

"I'll get your change," Tessa said a bit glumly, shoving his plate, silverware and coffee mug into the bin beneath the counter and picking up the bill.

"No need," Jesse said.

"That's too much," Tessa said. "The tip, I mean."

"You have your opinion," Jesse answered, "and I have mine."

Tessa sighed. She was attracted to this man, and she didn't like the idea one bit.

There were just too many red flags.

He'd won Isabel over all too easily. He was so far out of Tessa's orbit that he might as well have been from another planet, and he wasn't above using money, however small the amount, to get his way.

On top of all that, he apparently thought he was another John Wayne.

Better to shut this whole thing down before it got away from her, she decided.

She and Isabel would visit Bitter Gulch. They would eat whatever he meant to cook in the hotel kitchen.

And that would be it.

Done. Old news. *Finis.*

What a bummer.

Jesse waited until he was out of Bailey's and in the parking lot around the corner before he punched the air with one fist and grinned like the fool he was.

Eat your heart out, John Wayne. Jesse McKettrick just rode into town.

His jubilant mood was stupid, he decided, as he unlocked his truck and swung up into the driver's seat. It faded a little more when he remembered that he had no intention of staying in Painted Pony Creek, even though he'd come to love the place.

He'd left California—and his thriving law practice there—after two major events: his divorce from Cynthia and a sad break with a man he'd considered a true friend. Until Todd had married Jesse's ex-wife a month after the breakup was official, that was.

Both of them swore they hadn't been cheating, but Jesse was skeptical.

He'd moved to the Creek for a change of scene, and to get some perspective on his life, decide what he wanted to do next. He'd learned carpentry from his grandfather, and excelled at it, so his older brother, Liam, had contracted him to build Bitter Gulch in an out-of-the-way Montana town. A widower with two kids, Liam worked as an architect, and he'd made his fortune by the time he was thirty-five.

Liam was getting ready to retire to the Creek, finish raising his kids in a place where he felt simple living was still possible.

Soon enough, he'd be moving here with his children. In fact, he'd already built a house out in the countryside. It was a nice place, with an in-ground pool, a guesthouse and a sizable barn.

Jesse was bunking at the guesthouse.

It was fancy enough by itself, that guesthouse. State-of-the-art kitchen, three bedrooms, two baths and a powder room, the works.

Jesse kept his clothes and other necessary items there, and he slept there, most nights, but the truth was, he'd never actually settled in for the duration.

The arrangement, after all, was temporary.

Essentially, he was a drifter, just passing through. He'd be moving on as soon as Bitter Gulch was open for business, when Liam would run the place. So there was no sense getting attached to anything or anybody.

He wasn't a monk—he'd dated several women since he'd come here—but the divorce from Cynthia, reasonably amicable as it had been, had taken the proverbial wind out of his sails. He'd been content to build and supervise a hired crew for eighteen months or so, never giving the future much thought.

Then, one rainy night in August, Tessa showed up.

Shy, unassuming, *gorgeous* Tessa, with her shimmering chestnut hair and her sad, gentle brown eyes.

Something inside Jesse had shifted the moment he met her.

No, he wasn't rube enough to think it was love.

Infatuation, maybe. Lust, even. But not love.

Not the mature, lasting kind, anyway, like his parents shared.

And with one divorce behind him already, Jesse wasn't inclined to push his luck. After all, he'd thought he'd loved Cynthia—even now he considered her a friend—but, in the end, they hadn't been able to make it work.

They'd both wanted kids in the beginning—he still did, which might be part of the reason he was attracted to Tessa.

But Cynthia had changed her mind about starting a family about a week after they'd both passed the California Bar Exam and taken entry-level positions in the same high-profile firm.

To make matters worse, Jesse had realized pretty quickly, and with no little self-recrimination, that he'd rather run the McKettricks' thousand-acre cattle ranch than practice law. He'd hated wearing suits and ties every day, instead of the jeans and work shirts he was used to, having worked for his parents all through college and law school. And he'd missed working with his hands, riding fence lines and herding cattle, even bucking bales and digging postholes.

Cynthia, on the other hand, had gone into hyper-drive, relishing every moment of her new job.

She liked making up, dressing up and dazzling the firm's senior partners with her flair for interpreting the law and providing spot-on backup and thorough research in every case she helped with.

She was sorry if she'd given Jesse the wrong impression, she'd said.

"People change." She'd said that, too.

Jesse hadn't been angry, not at first.

But he'd sure as hell been disappointed.

Very, very disappointed.

For a while, they'd tried to hold on, he and Cynthia, but they'd soon realized the marriage, short as it was, had reached its expiration date.

They'd filed for a legal separation, split the few assets they'd managed to acquire during their five-year union and gone their own ways.

The divorce itself was a mere formality.

A nonevent.

Then, all of a sudden, Todd and Cynthia were dating, hot and heavy.

And they were married within six months.

Like the marriage, Jesse's longtime friendship with Todd was just too damn awkward to maintain.

Still, Jesse might have been all right with the situation—

eventually—if Cynthia hadn't gotten pregnant before a year had passed.

She'd admitted the pregnancy was a monumental accident, that she still didn't see herself as a mother, but she meant to have the child and make the best of things.

Cynthia was a grown woman, obviously, and what she did with her life, her body and her career was her own business, but Jesse, though out of love with her in no uncertain terms, had been devastated.

He'd worked hard to put it all behind him, and moving to the Creek had definitely helped. But he was remembering it when he pulled up in front of the guesthouse on his brother's place and shut off the truck's engine.

He sat still behind the wheel and shook off the sadness thoughts of Cynthia and her baby always brought on. She'd divorced Todd soon after the baby was born, hired a full-time nanny and thrown herself back into her brilliant career.

The whole thing had left Jesse's head spinning, even though he was glad he and Cynthia had divorced. What they'd had together, before the split, hadn't been true love; instead, it had been a combination of youthful lust, inexperience and poor judgment.

These days, he liked and respected Cynthia, though he and Todd were forever on the outs, and he was little Landry's godfather, a role he took seriously. Even relished.

It was beginning to look as though being a godfather was as close as he was going to get to being a dad himself.

Again, he thought of Tessa and her little girl.

Whoa back, cowboy, he told himself. *Don't get carried away*.

Good advice. After all, he'd practically roped and hog-tied the woman just to get her to spend an evening with him.

He got out of the truck and headed for the cottage behind Liam's sprawling house. He heard his dog barking a jubilant greeting from the other side of the front door, and smiled.

People were complicated, and that was a fact. Dogs, on the other hand, were simple and pure-hearted, utterly devoted to their person or persons—for life.

Jesse opened the door and stepped inside. The animal nearly knocked him off his feet, barking wildly and smiling in that way only dogs could smile, and Jesse laughed, ruffled the critter's floppy ears.

Norvel was a mixture of God knew how many breeds, but the Labs won out. His coat was a buff color, and his eyes were mismatched—one brown, one blue. Jesse had adopted him when he'd first arrived in

Painted Pony Creek, knowing no one and committed to a building project that was way above his pay grade.

Up until then, the most ambitious jobs he'd ever undertaken, when it came to carpentry at least, were building a chicken coop for his grandmother and putting a new roof on his mom's gazebo.

For some incomprehensible reason, Liam had trusted him to build what amounted to an entire *town*. Once Main Street was finished, a series of cabins would be added to accommodate weekend visitors and vacationers.

Liam, an architect by trade, had drawn up blueprints for all of it. Right down to the public restrooms designed to look like old-time privies.

Face-to-face with the reality of the task he'd undertaken, Jesse had decided he couldn't see this through alone, and he'd climbed into his truck and driven straight to the Creek's animal shelter. He no longer had a wife. He didn't have kids. So, damn it, he would have a dog.

He and Norvel had been best buddies from that day on.

Of course he'd made friends—he was reserved, not a recluse—but his dog was still the best of them all.

"Come on," he said, once Norvel had settled down a little. "You need a walk."

He didn't bother with a leash. Liam's property was

way out in the country, halfway between the Creek and the neighboring town of Silver Hills, and it was surrounded by open fields and seldom-used dirt roads.

Definitely dog friendly.

Norvel, who could have passed for a golden retriever in the right light, pranced alongside him, thrilled as always by the perfectly ordinary.

People, Jesse thought, could learn a lot from dogs.

❄ 3 ❄

Holding Isabel's mittened hand, Tessa paused on the broken sidewalk in front of her rental house, paying little attention to her child's excited chatter about Jesse McKettrick and the impending visit to Bitter Gulch.

I shouldn't have said yes, Tessa thought.

"Why are we just standing here, Mommy?" Isabel inquired. "It's cold."

Tessa rallied herself enough to squeeze Isabel's fingers lightly and smile. "I was just thinking that our house could use a coat of paint," she said, her tone deliberately casual. *Not to mention new floors, windows and bathroom fixtures.*

"I'll get the mail while you're thinking about paint," Isabel informed her, sounding very businesslike. She pulled her hand free of Tessa's and skipped to the old-fashioned mailbox on the edge of the front lawn.

Which was more of a weed patch than a lawn.

Tessa's spirits were slipping, and she scrambled to catch hold of them.

She should be grateful, she thought. The little house was no palace, but it was livable and the rent was cheap. The elderly owner, Harold Farriday, was easy to deal with, since he lived in Missoula in a retirement home, along with his wife, Evelyn. They cashed Tessa's rent checks, which always went out a week early, and never called or visited.

A thickness formed in Tessa's throat, nearly cutting off her breath, and her eyes prickled. No matter how she tried, or how hard she worked, things never seemed to get better.

Yes, she and Isabel had been essentially homeless when they'd come to the Creek three months before, and now Tessa had a steady job and they both had a home to live in.

She felt guilty for wanting more.

How much was enough, for heaven's sake?

"Mommy," Isabel prompted, beside her again, holding a large manila envelope out to her. "We got some mail!"

Tessa took the envelope, thanked her daughter and didn't bother to open the packet. It was probably a catalog or a flyer.

Therefore, she tucked it under her elbow and extended a hand to Isabel. "Let's get inside where it's warm, kiddo," she said, and they made their way up the lumpy brick walk leading to the front door, being careful to pick up their feet, since it would be easy to trip and fall if they didn't pay attention.

All they needed, she thought ruefully as she worked the key in the old-fashioned lock, struggling a little, would be broken bones. Moreover, now that the weather was getting colder, the whole mechanism might freeze.

Once inside, Isabel set aside her turkey artwork and wrestled out of her coat.

It wasn't raggedy, that coat, even though Tessa had bought it at a secondhand shop back in Omaha, but Isabel had grown since the purchase, and that meant the garment was a little tighter than it should be, and short in the sleeves.

Shedding her own coat, nipped in at the waist, long and fashioned of bright red wool, Tessa shivered slightly and rubbed her upper arms. Her coat, like Isabel's, came from a thrift store, as had the majority of their clothes.

Tessa loved that coat; a rare find with a ten-dollar price tag, it was classically cut, with three large black buttons in front. She took good care of it, and it still looked relatively new.

Plus, it was warm.

Once their outerwear had been hung on the ancient coat-tree beside the entrance, Tessa crossed to the woodstove. She opened its glass-fronted door, struck a match from the box on the shelf that served as a sort of mantel and lit the wadded newspaper and kindling inside.

A fire leaped up, surprising Tessa a little, as it always did. She'd lit the stove for atmosphere, mostly—she loved the smell, the merry crackle, the warmth—since the old house boasted a furnace powered by natural gas.

A man named Mitch had driven up in a flatbed truck loaded with firewood a day or two after Tessa and Isabel had moved here from the apartment above Bailey's. He'd said he worked for Cord and Shallie Hollister on their sprawling ranch, and had refused payment for the wood. Which was fortunate, since Tessa had just paid her first month's rent and security deposit, and had almost zero money left.

Other people had visited, welcoming her and her

child to town with casseroles, quilts, pots and pans—
even an old but functional washer and dryer.

It was crazy, in a wonderful way, how Painted Pony
Creek had embraced the newcomers. In all her travels,
which were considerable, she'd never encountered such
easy, down-home friendliness.

Isabel interrupted Tessa's thoughts then, with a bright,
"What are we going to wear on our date with Jesse?"

Tessa paused, about to head for the kitchen and make
tea. "That's Mr. McKettrick to you, young lady, until
he says otherwise. And you're *way* too young to date."

"We were *both* invited," Isabel pointed out.

"Yes, we were."

"So it's a date."

"It's a tour of Bitter Gulch and supper in the hotel
kitchen. *Not* exactly a 'date.'"

"I want to wear my princess costume," Isabel said, undaunted. "I look pretty in it, and I like the tiara."

"You look pretty in everything," Tessa replied, in motion again.

Reaching the tiny kitchen with its sloping floors, farm-
house sink and cheery red-and-white-checked curtains—
bought at Walmart, on clearance—Tessa filled the copper
teakettle with good rural Montana water and set it on the

stove. She turned on a gas burner and bent slightly to adjust the blue flame.

"You only say that because you're my mommy and you love me," Isabel said. She was busy finding a place on the front of the refrigerator to tape up her artwork.

"Of course I love you," Tessa answered. "Are you hungry?"

"We're going to Bitter Gulch for supper," Isabel reminded her, turning from the fluttering plethora of drawings and schedules and school papers to meet her mother's eyes. "We shouldn't spoil our appetite."

"I don't think a fruit cup and a stick of string cheese will make you too full to handle supper," Tessa said reasonably. "It will be at least two and a half hours before we eat. So how about you have a snack and then lie down for an hour or so. You don't want to show up sleepy, I'm sure."

Isabel considered her prospects solemnly, then smiled a sunshine smile. "Can I wear the princess dress?"

Tessa sighed. "Don't you think jeans and a sweatshirt would be more fitting? I don't recall seeing a single princess in any of the Western movies we've watched."

The first puff of steam shot from the teakettle, and the water inside gurgled. Tessa dropped a tea bag into her favorite mug, set it on the warped counter, which

was topped in very old green linoleum, and went to
the fridge for Isabel's snack.

"Wash your hands first," Tessa instructed, out of
habit rather than necessity. Isabel was a very conscientious child—maybe *too* conscientious for someone
so young.

Tessa fretted inwardly, and certainly not for the first
time, that the vagabond, lick-and-a-prayer way they'd
been living might have harmed Isabel in some funda-
mental way. She'd always tried to frame it as an adventure, and Isabel usually played along.

Still, it wasn't normal, spending so much time on the
road, having to move on so often like a pair of fugitives.

In a way, they *were* fugitives, because Marjory Laughlin
had decided she wanted custody less than a month after
Tessa had given birth.

First the older woman had filed for visitation privi-
leges, claiming grandparents' rights. Because Brent had
signed documents forfeiting all personal or legal claim
to his daughter, and probably didn't want to encounter
her on forays to the family's Back Bay mansion, he'd
managed to talk his stepmother into dropping her case.

For a while, Marjory had subsided.

Then, as Tessa learned from a friend, when Brent
apparently confided in Marjory that he'd had a vasec-

tomy to avoid fathering a second unwanted child, the grande dame had absolutely lost it.

She'd begun playing mind games with Tessa, gas-lighting from a distance.

And then, when Isabel was barely two years old, Marjory had attempted to kidnap the child from a Kansas City day care center.

There had been threats, too, but Marjory was a very clever narcissist with plenty of resources, and Tessa's complaints to the police were discounted as hearsay.

At least one of Brent's stepmother's motives must have been greed; the Laughlin fortune equaled the gross national product of some small countries, and as the only child, Brent was the sole heir. As things stood, if something happened to him, everything would be held in trust for Isabel.

Therefore, Marjory wanted to be in charge of the child, 24/7—forever.

Even without the evil-stepmother factor, the amount of the estate was staggering and, frankly, Tessa didn't want her daughter to be saddled with the responsibility, or the expectations and demands, such a huge amount of money would bring with it, even as an adult. The fund Brent had set up to cover Isabel's higher education was plenty.

But Marjory was, in a word, crazy.

Stone-cold, raving, batshit crazy.

She'd been on a rampage ever since Brent's announcement, and even though she'd been unsuccessful in court regarding access to her infant granddaughter, she obviously hadn't given up.

Besides all the behind-the-scenes subterfuge, the woman just kept hiring new lawyers, and she was still trying to prove Tessa unfit to parent a Laughlin child. She'd had Tessa's background investigated and learned that she'd been abandoned in front of a movie theater at the age of eight. That her bipolar mother had died of an opiate overdose a year later. That until she'd aged out of the system at eighteen, Tessa had been raised in a series of foster homes.

The last and best of those had belonged to a childless couple named Paul and Rachel Stafford. Tessa had been with the Staffords for five years, and while they hadn't legally adopted her, they'd considered her their own. They were people of modest means—home was an old but well-maintained double-wide—and they'd been good to Tessa.

In fact, they'd loved her.

After high school, they'd encouraged her to attend the local junior college and allowed her to remain a part of their household. She'd taken a part-time job at a bowling alley and started school, planning to switch to a four-year college later and earn a degree in education.

Two things had happened to change the course of Tessa's life.

First, the Staffords had been killed in an automobile accident before she'd finished her freshman year. And second, she'd met Brent Laughlin at a party, jettisoned all good sense out of sheer loneliness and let him talk her into becoming his secret girlfriend.

Secret, because he didn't want his venerable family to know she existed.

Talk about a red flag.

Grief-stricken by the loss of her foster parents, hidden from practically everyone Brent knew as though she were somehow shameful, and eventually blindsided by a pregnancy she'd taken every precaution to avoid, Tessa had been forced to drop out of school, at least for the time being.

She and Brent were over by then.

So over.

But Brent's stepmother had found out about Isabel, and that her stepson, sole heir to the Laughlin fortune, had turned himself from a stallion into a gelding.

Furious, she'd tracked Tessa down, made a huge scene

in the dress shop where she worked part-time and got-ten Tessa fired. At least she still had her bartending job at a nightclub. But the whole thing had been a crap-storm, and for all the barriers Marjory had encountered in her quest to claim and raise her supposed grandchild, she wouldn't back off.

Social media buzzed with her vicious attacks on Tessa's character.

Soon enough, Tessa had figured—and believed still—Marjory would try to snatch Isabel again and attempt to take her out of the country, out of Tessa's reach. She might have legal custody, but the Laughlins had money—vast sums of it, dating back to New England's whaling days—and an army of contacts, some but not all of whom were law-abiding citizens.

The very thought of what could happen was terri-fying.

"Mommy!" Isabel shouted, breaking into Tessa's fear-fugue. "The teakettle is boiling over!"

Tessa came to her senses with a jolt, hurried to move the kettle off the burner and quell the flame, close to tears.

Then she dropped into a chair and covered her face with both hands, trying to breathe slowly and evenly. Maybe, she thought, she had been a fool to think she and Isabel could make a home in Painted Pony Creek, Montana.

They should have moved on as soon as she'd gotten her car fixed and saved a bit for gas and food.

Instead, they'd stayed.

Tessa had landed a job she liked, working with people she liked.

She had friends for the first time in too long, and so did Isabel. The little girl loved kindergarten and afternoon day care. She had all the playdates she could handle, and a part in the Christmas pageant.

Tessa sat numbly in her chair, shaking her head at her own stupidity.

She'd made a terrible mistake, staying in Painted Pony Creek.

Isabel huddled close, then maneuvered herself onto Tessa's lap. "You look sad, Mommy. Aren't you happy that we get to go to Bitter Gulch?" She paused, her blue eyes earnest as she studied her mother's carefully controlled face. "It'll be lots of fun, and J—Mr. McKettrick is a really nice man."

Tessa sniffled, rested her forehead against Isabel's and gave a watery smile. God, she was tired of always having to be brave.

Just once, she wanted to yell, stomp her feet, throw things—let out all her frustration and fury.

She also wanted to find Marjory Laughlin and beat the ever-loving crap out of her.

She drew a deep, somewhat shaky breath.

Steadied herself.

"Finish your snack," she told her little girl. "If you rest for an hour—you don't even have to sleep, just take your shoes off and lie on your bed—I'll let you wear your princess dress tonight."

Isabel's face was suddenly luminous. Someday, she'd be a beauty.

Mentally, Tessa planted herself firmly in the present. "Someday" would take care of itself. Her focus had to be "now."

She wanted to flee again, but she had to keep that from Isabel, who was so happy in the friendly little town.

The realization that another, more courageous side of her wanted to stay, to stand her ground, struck her with the suddenness and impact of a ball of heat lightning.

She was tired of making decisions from a place of fear, tired of playing Marjory's sinister games.

Suppose they *didn't* move on this time?

Suppose, instead, Tessa dug in her heels and fought back?

She'd been cowardly long enough.

It was time to bring out her inner Mama Bear, for sure.

And if Medusa showed up, Tessa would stand up to her.

Fiercely.

This town ain't big enough for the both of us, pardner, she thought, in the spirit of all things Western.

And then she laughed.

Approximately two and a half hours later, Jesse rapped lightly at the door.

Isabel, clad in her erstwhile Halloween costume, a froth of pink netting and rhinestones, crowned by her plastic tiara, rushed to admit him.

"Come in!" she crowed.

Jesse stepped over the threshold, caught Tessa's eye—she was standing in the kitchen doorway, clad in her best casual outfit, black jeans and matching sweater—and winked.

Then, closing the door behind him, he took in Isabel's costume.

"You didn't tell me you were royalty," he remarked solemnly, looking down at his own jeans, white shirt and denim jacket. "I would have worn better boots."

Isabel beamed, taking in Jesse's attention as though it were life-giving.

Maybe, for her, a fatherless child, it was.

That gave Tessa a pang. She was a good mother, and she knew Isabel felt secure in her love—she'd made every effort to convey the message to her little girl from infancy on—but she knew her daughter secretly wanted a daddy.

As a little girl, *she* certainly had.

Don't go there, Tessa warned herself, always on the alert for thoughts that could lead her back down the rabbit hole—and hadn't she just had to climb out of it a little while ago.

This is no big deal, the rational part of her brain assured her.

"The hell it isn't," Tessa murmured under her breath.

"I'm not royalty," Isabel asserted. "I'm a *princess*."

Jesse pondered the dichotomy. "All righty then, Your Highness."

"I'm *Princess Isabel*," the child asserted. "But you can just call me Isabel."

"Thank you," Jesse said formally.

His eyes were dancing with amusement when he raised his gaze to Tessa again.

"Ready?" he asked.

"Ready," Tessa lied.

He helped her into her good coat, and because he was standing behind her by then, and she'd pinned her

shoulder-length brown hair up in a loose bun, she felt
his breath against her nape.

Soon, they were all inside his flashy truck. Judging by
the dashboard and all its modern features, the vehicle was
new and top-of-the-line. It boasted a roomy back seat and
even a proper car seat, into which he had buckled Princess
Isabel before climbing into the driver's seat.

"You have kids?" Tessa asked, nodding to the special safety equipment where Isabel perched, tiara askew,
looking thrilled.

Jesse grinned. "Unfortunately not," he replied. "The
car seat belongs to my godson. I usually spend some
time with him whenever I go home."

"Where's home?" she asked, as he started the engine.
That the Creek wasn't home to him was unsettling,
though Tessa couldn't have said why exactly.

"A little town just north of Los Angeles. My folks
own a ranch there."

Tessa shifted her attention to the fancy dashboard.

USB ports. Speakers. Buttons and knobs.

Her own car, moldering in the teetering attached
garage behind the rental house, hadn't run since the
night it had given out alongside a country road. She
couldn't afford to fix it.

"So if Los Angeles is home…?"

"Not Los Angeles," Jesse said mildly when Tessa's voice trailed off. "The town's called Olive Grove."

They were rolling along the side streets, familiar scenery slipping past on all sides.

"Olive Grove. Named for obvious reasons, I suppose?" Tessa ventured. It was easy, making small talk with Jesse.

He laughed. "Yeah," he answered. "We grow a mean olive in those parts."

"Is that what your parents raise on the ranch?" *A rancher.* Until she'd come to the Creek, where ranchers and farmers were plentiful, she'd never met one.

Jesse nodded. "Among other things. We have a vineyard, too, and cattle. A *lot* of cattle."

"I'm impressed."

"Don't be—not on my account, anyway. My parents own the ranch, and they run the place with some help from my younger brother, Rhett—we call him Rowdy most of the time and not without reason." Jesse's tone was fond.

"And you build Western towns?"

He nodded again. "Yes," he said. "Though it's not my career. I'm a lawyer, on temporary sabbatical."

As little as Tessa knew about Jesse, from what she could glean serving him at Bailey's on occasion, she had known he was an attorney—her coworker Miranda had told her that much, also mentioning that he was single.

The ranch hadn't been mentioned, at least to Tessa.

Nor had the vineyards, the olive groves and the cattle.

They were turning onto Main Street by then, passing between Bailey's and the hardware store.

"Hello, turkey!" Isabel shouted, leaning in the sturdy car seat to peer out the window and probably wave.

Tessa and Jesse both started at the sound.

Both laughed.

"Isabel," Tessa said after a few moments of recovery. "Indoor voice."

"But we're not *really* indoors," Isabel protested good-naturedly. "We're in a *truck*, silly."

"Whatever," Tessa replied briskly. "Don't yell like that again, please. You scared me half to death."

Isabel merely sighed.

Soon, they were passing Brynne Garrett's lodge. She was Alice Bailey's daughter, and Tessa had gotten to know her a little and liked her. Brynne, married to Sheriff Eli Garrett and the mother of twin boys and a brand-new baby girl named Sierra, helped out at the restaurant and bar sometimes. Though not as often now, since she'd given birth. Plus, she had her own thriving business to look after. The lodge served as an art school, a B & B and a wedding venue.

Just beyond the parklike venue, with its many trees and its rolling landscape, stood the very mysterious construction site, where Bitter Gulch was being built.

It was surrounded by high fences and lined with tarps, which made it impossible to see inside.

That was part of the fun. Only the construction workers and a few others had seen the inside. The unveiling, come summer, would be a *very* big deal, not only in Painted Pony Creek, but for miles around.

As they pulled up in front of a massive gate, Isabel was practically jumping up and down in her car seat, she was so excited.

"*This*," she blurted, "is the best thing *ever*!"

Jesse chuckled and climbed out of the truck to unlock the gate, which bore a variety of signs saying things like, No Unauthorized Admittance and No Phones, No Cameras.

Tessa felt a frisson of excitement of her own, though it had more to do with Jesse McKettrick than the prospect of getting an early glimpse of the future tourist attraction.

The gate swung open with a push from Jesse, and he returned to the truck.

"Sometimes," he confided to Tessa, "I think I've spent most of my life opening and closing gates. First on the ranch, and now here."

Tessa smiled. "I'll bet," she replied, leaning forward to peer through the windshield at the two rows of authentic-looking buildings, facing each other across a wide dirt street.

Jesse parked the truck, got out and closed the gate behind them.

Isabel was still bouncing. "*Nobody* at kindergarten *or* day care has *ever* been to Bitter Gulch!" she blurted out. "I'm the very, very *first* Painted Pony Creek kid to come here!"

Again, Tessa smiled. Exciting experiences like this one were rare in Isabel's young life, and in hers. She would tuck this evening away in a corner of her mind, like the treasure it was. That way, when times got tough again, as they always did, she could bring the memory out and savor it, like a shiny good-luck piece or a pretty river rock.

The tour of the town was quick, since most of the buildings were unfinished, except for their facades.

The streetlights Jesse had promised had come on with the flip of a lever, and that moment was magical to Isabel, and even Tessa.

There was a marshal's office, a saloon, a bank, a general store, a blacksmith's shop, a livery stable and, of course, the hotel, among other nineteenth-century amenities, as well as a church at the far end of the long street.

The street itself was lined with hitching rails and wooden water troughs—still empty—and the sidewalks were wooden. Tessa could almost hear the thump of boot heels and the clink of spurs.

"Wow!" Isabel cried repeatedly.

It was getting chilly, and the hotel, the only structure lit up from within, grew more inviting.

"Will there be a brothel above the saloon?" Tessa asked when Isabel was out of earshot.

He chuckled. "In name only. There *will* be dancehall girls, though, and probably a madam. All part of the show."

Isabel was standing in front of the desk when they entered; the moment Jesse had opened one of the hotel's double doors, the little girl had rushed inside.

Jesse waited, held the door open for Tessa. Resting his hand lightly and briefly on the small of her back as she stepped over the threshold ahead of him.

She loved the sheer masculinity of that gesture. Loved being touched by Jesse McKettrick, though she shook that thought off quickly. She'd fallen under a man's spell once before, and it had been disastrous, except for Isabel.

Her baby girl made all that hassle worthwhile.

The hotel lobby was straight out of an old movie— wooden reception desk with a big book atop it, cubby-holes behind, each with a large brass key dangling from an inside hook. There were elegant round tables, colorful Turkish rugs, gas-light fixtures.

A wide stairway arched upward to the second floor.

"How many rooms?" Tessa asked, intrigued.

"Ten," Jesse answered. "Plus two suites."

She marveled. "All this was your idea?"

"Nope," Jesse replied, without apparent concern. "Bitter Gulch is my brother Liam's baby. I'm just here to hammer in a few nails and oversee the guys who actually know what they're doing."

"It's quite a project," Tessa said, wondering why an attorney would interrupt his law career to build something like this, spectacular though it was.

"Yep," Jesse agreed. "It's meant to be a tourist attraction, but Liam's already signed with a few movie producers who want to shoot here."

"People are going to film movies here?" Tessa asked, and then felt stupid. The man had just said that was going to happen. "*That's* going to draw crowds."

By then, Jesse was ushering her through a high, or-
nately decorated archway into a full formal dining
room, complete with tables and chairs. The walls were
lined with mirrors and garish paintings of voluptuous
women, and more tasteful landscapes, which looked
like Brynne Garrett's work.

"That's the idea," Jesse said. He gestured toward an
inside door.

Isabel was standing in the middle of the dining room,
her head tilted back, admiring the exquisite chandelier overhead.

She looked so cute, in her princess dress, her sneakers,
her too-small coat. The tiara, studded with tacky plastic
gems, dangled from her right hand.

A tsunami of love for her child washed over Tessa.

Jesse must have been watching her face, because he
murmured, "You're a very lucky woman, Tessa Stafford."

Tessa's eyes burned, and her throat tightened. She
nodded. "Yes," she replied. "I am."

"This way to the grub, Princess Isabel," he called.

Isabel's chandelier spell was broken, and she rushed
toward Jesse and Tessa, beaming.

"This place is like a *castle*!" she cried.

"Fit for a princess," Jesse replied gently, touching the

top of Isabel's blond head when she reached them. Then, after a pause, he went on. "Next stop, the kitchen."

It was a spacious room, that kitchen, and though it boasted a gleaming cast-iron stove, trimmed in bright chrome, there was also a commercial-grade eight-burner gas counterpart, a separate grill and a large sub-zero refrigerator.

A round wooden table sat in the center of the kitchen, set for three.

"Is there a place to wash up?" Tessa asked somewhat meekly. There was an enormous stainless-steel sink next to the chef's stove, but Isabel wouldn't be able to reach, and besides, the thing was kind of intimidating.

No one touches me but Gordon Ramsay, it seemed to say.

Jesse cocked a thumb toward two doors. "The one on the right is a powder room," he said, taking off his coat.

"What's the one on the left?" Isabel asked, always a bit nosy.

"The pantry," Jesse informed her lightly. He hung the coat on one of several hooks behind the kitchen door, and then he helped Tessa and Isabel out of theirs and hung those up, too.

The powder room was strictly modern, which came as a relief to Tessa. By then, she was on sensory overload.

When they returned, Jesse was standing in front of

the big sink, drying his hands on a kitchen towel. Like a waiter in a very fancy restaurant, he went to the table and drew back Tessa's chair. Once she was seated, he did the same for Isabel.

"I hope you like hamburgers," he said.

Both Tessa and Isabel nodded.

Jesse took a supermarket vegetable tray from the fridge, removed the lid and set it in the center of the table.

"Munch away. The burgers will take about twenty minutes."

While Isabel and Tessa noshed on carrots, celery and small spears of broccoli, Jesse cooked.

The kitchen smelled heavenly.

Tessa's stomach rumbled.

And Princess Isabel fell asleep in her chair.

❄ 4 ❄

Tessa's whispered offers to help with the after-supper cleanup were met with Jesse's firm refusal.

"I'll come back and do all that later, after I've taken you and the princess home," he said.

There was clearly no point in arguing.

Jesse put on his coat, helped Tessa into her own and watched as Tessa woke Isabel just long enough to get her into her jacket. The little girl had had a big evening, and, try though she might to stay awake, she kept nodding off.

Tessa was about to lift the child into her arms when Jesse interceded.

"May I?" he asked.

The man was *so* polite. He was either a genuinely good person or a very talented actor.

If he turned out to be a jerk, Tessa was going to lose faith in humanity.

"I— Sure," Tessa said. "I guess."

Gently, he lifted Isabel from her chair.

She woke, but immediately dropped off to sleep again, resting her head on Jesse's shoulder.

He held the child in an easy, practiced way, and something about the sight caused a sweet pinch deep in Tessa's wary heart.

Be careful, she warned herself. *This is a slippery slope.*

Isabel woke up when they reached the truck, and Jesse fastened her into the car seat. "Mommy?" she murmured.

"Right here," Tessa told her, turning in the passenger seat to look at the child.

Isabel sighed and went back to sleep.

Jesse went to open the gate, then got back in.

And turned to face Tessa.

"That's one great kid you have there," he said quietly, and his voice sounded a little gruff to Tessa. Authentic emotion—or acting?

He probably deserved the benefit of the doubt, but

Tessa had been badly burned and that made her cautious.

And possibly screwed up.

"Thank you," she replied after clearing her own throat. "I think so, too."

Jesse looked as though he wanted to say more, but he must have decided against it, because he just started the engine and drove through the gate. He stopped to close and lock it again, then came back to the truck.

"Question for a question?" Tessa ventured, uncomfortable even though the silence was strangely easy. "Like a trade?"

"Ladies first," Jesse replied, glancing at her but then turning his gaze back to the road.

"You clearly love children. Why don't you have any?"

He was silent for a long moment, and it seemed to Tessa that his jawline hardened, though briefly. "I wanted them, but apparently that wasn't the plan."

There was regret in his voice, and a measure of pain. Maybe he was as bad at relationships as Tessa was.

"Okay," she said, somewhat at a loss.

The headlights splashed over the road ahead.

"My turn?"

Tessa suppressed a sigh. "Your turn," she confirmed.

"What—or who—are you running away from?"

Tessa hadn't expected that. "What makes you think I'm running away from something?"

"Unfair. That's a question, not an answer."

"I'm not a fugitive, if that's what you want to know," Tessa said, trying to sound amused.

"Not quite an answer," Jesse pointed out.

"You *are* a lawyer," Tessa remarked.

Jesse laughed; the sound was low and a little hoarse. "And a good one," he said.

"Why are you building a movie set–tourist attraction instead of practicing law?" she asked.

"Is it your turn?" he countered with a note of amusement in his voice.

"Yes. And don't try to trick me by asking another question instead of answering," Tessa said with a boldness that amazed her.

Jesse's reasons for working in construction instead of practicing law were his own business. He'd be well within his rights to tell her to take a flying leap.

"You wouldn't make a bad lawyer yourself," he told her.

They were nearing Tessa's house now.

"I'm what I'm qualified to be—a service worker in a restaurant."

"What's wrong with that?"

Tessa stumbled over that question. "Nothing, of course. I like my job."

"But?"

"But if I had a law degree I would use it."

"Would you now?"

This conversation was getting them nowhere.

When Tessa didn't say anything, Jesse pressed the issue.

"I know you've got to be careful, Tessa," he said. "What I've been trying to say is that I'm not out to hurt you. I'm far from perfect, but I'm probably better than you think I am."

They'd reached the rental house, and Jesse pulled the truck to a stop in front. Without another word, he got out of the vehicle, came around to open Tessa's door for her, then collected Isabel from the car seat.

As before, the little girl simply sighed and rested her head on Jesse's shoulder. She was clasping her tiara in one hand, and Tessa took it from her, tucked it into the deep pocket of her coat.

This time around, Jesse didn't ask Tessa's permission to carry her child.

He stepped back to let her precede him up the walk

and onto the porch, and as she wrestled with the ancient lock, he waited, saying nothing.

Tessa stepped into her tiny living room, and Jesse followed.

"Stay for coffee?" she asked against her better judgment.

Jesse looked pleased, and a little relieved, though she had to look closely to notice. "I'd like that," he said.

"Good," she replied, pleased and relieved herself. She took her sleeping child from Jesse's arms, held her close. "I'll put the princess to bed and be back in a few minutes."

"Okay," Jesse said. After a moment of hesitation, he shrugged out of his coat, hung it on the coat-tree.

He seemed too big to be inside Tessa's humble little house. The walls were ready to bulge and expand in order to accommodate him.

"Have a seat anywhere you like," Tessa urged. With that, she blushed and hurried away.

In the bathroom, she held the sleepy princess up long enough to brush her teeth and wash her face, and when that was done, she pointed to the toilet and whispered, "Pee."

Isabel complied.

Tessa washed her daughter's hands afterward and led

her into the closet-size chamber that passed as Isabel's bedroom.

"Say your prayers," Tessa instructed after tucking Isabel in and planting a noisy kiss on her forehead.

Isabel's eyelids fluttered. "Thank you, God," she mumbled, leaving long gaps between the words, "for Bitter Gulch and Mommy. Amen."

Tessa smiled and kissed the child again.

Playing second fiddle to an Old West town, she thought, slipping out of Isabel's room and closing the door quietly behind her.

The scent of coffee brewing caught her attention, drew her into the kitchen.

"I figured you'd want decaf at this hour," Jesse said, holding out a steaming cup. Then he poured a cup for himself and joined Tessa at the table, where she'd collapsed into a chair, suddenly exhausted.

She imagined crawling between cold sheets after Jesse left, and shivered at the thought, even as she took her first sip of coffee.

One of the things Tessa missed most about having a man in her life was being held before sleep, feeling warm and safe and cared-for in strong arms.

And look where that got you, she thought glumly.

Seated across from her, Jesse narrowed his eyes. "What's going through your mind right now, Ms. Stafford?"

"That I should be careful," she answered.

Jesse sighed. "You must have been burned very badly," he said.

There was no use in beating around the proverbial bush. "I was," she answered. "His name is Brent and he's a card-carrying pr—jerk. But the sad truth is, I burned myself. I fell for his song-and-dance routine. I was so eager to live the dream, I missed all the red flags."

"You're divorced, then?" Jesse put the question cautiously.

Tessa shook her head. Set her coffee cup down, because her hands were shaking, too. She shouldn't be spilling her guts like this, but, well, it felt pretty good. Even a little cozy.

"Brent wouldn't stoop to marry the likes of me," she said without self-pity. "I grew up in foster homes, after my mother decided eight years of her hit-and-miss care were enough. I certainly wasn't sheltered—I don't have that excuse—but I was ridiculously naive, just the same."

Jesse's eyes darkened. "That's rough," he said after a long time.

"Lots of people have it worse," Tessa replied. That was her private mantra, had been for a long time.

"Lots of people have it better, too," Jesse pointed out, his coffee forgotten in front of him. He probably didn't drink decaf; he was just being polite.

At Bailey's, he always drank regular coffee, strong and black.

"Like you, for instance?"

"Like me," he said.

Tessa blew out a breath, palmed her forehead. "I'm sorry, Jesse. That was uncalled for."

A long but not uncomfortable silence fell between them.

Tessa kept expecting Jesse to get up and walk out, but he didn't.

"If we're going to get to know each other," he said finally, "we have to talk."

"There's too much to say," Tessa said wearily. "And most of it is stuff I should keep to myself."

"Why?"

"Because it's—embarrassing. And because we're so different, you and I. You come from a wonderful home, from the sounds of it. I, on the other hand, come from the system. You have a degree, and I—well—I don't."

"That's not a bad thing, Tessa," he replied. "I know

lots of happy, healthy and successful people who don't have a diploma from any college."

"You're just saying that."

"One thing you're going to learn about me is that I don't make small talk. And I mean everything I say. No point in saying it otherwise, now is there?"

"Probably not," Tessa conceded. "Did you plan on becoming a lawyer, growing up?"

"No. I planned on being Wyatt Earp, until I realized the job was taken."

Tessa laughed, then sobered a little. "My life isn't easy, Jesse. I have Isabel to think about. I have to work, and my money goes toward buying food and paying rent." She gestured so vigorously at her surroundings that she nearly spilled her coffee. "Making it from one day to the next is pretty much the best I can manage."

"So you never have time for yourself?" Jesse argued, not unkindly. "That sounds a little grim."

"That, if you'll forgive me for saying so, is easy for you to say, Jesse McKettrick," Tessa answered with spirit.

"Shh," Jesse said, pushing back his chair. "You'll wake Isabel."

There it was. He was up and on his feet. He was walking out.

And it was her own fault for letting the conversation veer off into the whys and wherefores of her messed-up life.

But he didn't walk out.

He rounded the table and drew Tessa to her feet.

"You," he breathed, "are beyond beautiful."

Then he pulled her into a loose embrace and took the pins from her hair, watched as it tumbled down around her shoulders.

She gazed up at him, helpless, stricken with an impossible desire to hold and be held by this man and no other. Ever.

Jesse crooked a calloused finger under her chin, lifted, looked directly into her eyes. "When you stop beating yourself up, Ms. Stafford, you are going to be a force to be reckoned with."

She couldn't speak. She could only stare up at him and hope she wouldn't hyperventilate.

Where were those brown paper bags she used for Isabel's lunch, anyway?

"I'd like very much to kiss you, Tessa. Right here and right now."

A tremor went through her, but she made no move to pull away.

"That scares you?" he asked, barely breathing the words.

"No. Yes. I don't—"

He kissed her then, tenderly at first, but then she pressed into him and encircled his neck with her arms, with a kind of controlled passion that made her want to lead him straight to her bed.

When the kiss ended, Tessa was breathless. Shaken to her core—which seemed molten.

Isabel was in the house, she reminded herself. Nothing could happen between her and Jesse, not now.

"I'm not on birth control," she blurted, and then blushed furiously.

Jesse brushed his lips lightly across her forehead. "You might want to take care of that in the next little while," he drawled. He wove his fingers through her hair, very gently. "In the meantime, there's no hurry. We need to get acquainted."

Get acquainted? One semi-date with this man and she was ready to hit the sheets. Why, if it hadn't been for Isabel, sleeping so innocently in her little bedroom—

"You're right," she heard herself say.

Jesse chuckled, kissed her again, this time with all the force of a butterfly's wing. "The Thanksgiving dance is next Saturday night, at the community center. Will you be my date, Tessa?"

"I'll have to fight my daughter for the privilege," Tessa said, trying to lighten the atmosphere a little. She was dizzy, overheated, even on a cold November night. "She's smitten with you."

"You think it's a privilege to go out with me?" Jesse teased.

Tessa grinned up at him. "Don't get too full of yourself," she replied. "I'm saying yes, and that's a big deal for me."

"It's a big deal for me, too," Jesse admitted.

And then he kissed her again, so thoroughly and so deeply that if he hadn't been holding her in his arms, she might have melted onto the linoleum like so much candle wax.

The next day, Tessa was off work. Her days on rotated, week by week.

She hummed under her breath that icy-bright morning, as she prepared oatmeal for Isabel's breakfast.

"You're happy today, Mommy," the little girl remarked, seated at the table. She practically sparkled, with her face scrubbed and her eyes shining. Dressed for school in a pink sweater and corduroy pants, she was ready for the day.

"I am," Tessa replied, stirring the oatmeal and looking back over one shoulder at her daughter. "I'm definitely happy. What about you?"

The power of the child's grin practically knocked Tessa off her feet. "I'm *super* happy!" she replied. "Today, I get to tell the *whole world* that I've been to Bitter Gulch!"

Tessa laughed, took the saucepan off the stove, picked up a serving spoon and dolloped a generous portion of oatmeal into a blue cereal bowl. "That might not be the way to win friends and influence people, kiddo."

"I already have friends, Mommy. I have Eleanor Susan Gwendolyn Gray, plus Sally and Michael and Jose and Henry."

Tessa set the bowl in front of her daughter, along with a spoon and a small pitcher of milk. She fetched blueberries from the refrigerator—no sugar allowed, at least at the beginning of the day.

"I know, buttercup," she said. "I just want you to think about how you would feel if any of your friends had been to Bitter Gulch and you hadn't."

"I'd be happy for them," Isabel insisted.

"You wouldn't feel jealous at all? Not even a little bit?"

Isabel considered. As usual, she spoke with the wisdom of someone far beyond her years. "Not if they didn't get all braggy and stuff, and try to make me feel left out."

"Right. Of course you want to tell your friends about your visit to Bitter Gulch. That's normal, and your prerogative—or your choice to make—and that's fine. Just be kind about it. Think about how you'd feel in their place."

Isabel rolled her eyes, looking for all the world like a miniature teenager. "I'm not a mean girl, Mommy," she said reproachfully.

"I know you're not," Tessa responded, filling a bowl with oatmeal for herself and carrying it to the table, where she sat down across from her daughter. "But an occasional reminder never hurts."

"I'll be good, Mommy," Isabel promised earnestly. "What are you going to do today?"

"Housework, laundry—maybe a quick trip to Vintage Treasures."

"Why would you go there?"

"Why do I usually go there?"

"To buy stuff."

"Right."

"What are you going to buy?"

Tessa intended to check out the selection of toys she

might place under the tree on Christmas Eve, though of course she didn't mention that. Isabel still believed in Santa Claus, after all. Probably a down-on-his-luck version of the jolly old man, since she received mostly used items.

Not that she remembered Christmases before last year, when she'd been four.

Now that Isabel was a little older—and far more aware than most five-year-olds—Tessa was going to have to up her game. Look for offerings in the almost-new category.

"I'm hoping to find a nice dress," she replied honestly. The little black number she'd been defaulting to for the last few years was beginning to look bedraggled.

Not that she'd had many actual dates since Isabel was born. Four or five, at most, and they'd all led straight to nowhere.

Isabel studied her. "Are you going on another date with Mr. McKettrick?"

She shouldn't have been surprised by the accuracy of her daughter's guess—it was common enough with Isabel—but she was.

She definitely was.

"Yes," she admitted with reluctance. She didn't want Isabel getting her hopes up, thinking she might end up with a father. "He asked me to the Thanksgiving dance."

Isabel ruminated. "Who's going to babysit me?" she wanted to know.

That was a worry.

Given the situation with Marjory, Tessa was very careful when it came to hiring babysitters. "Possibly Hayley Worth, if she's available. Or one of Chief Summers's daughters."

With the holiday season beginning, it might not be so easy to find someone. Hayley was a high school senior, a beautiful, intelligent girl, and she probably had a date of her own for the dance. Same with Melba's very popular daughters.

Carly Hollister was a possibility, if she happened to be home from college, but she, too, would most likely have other plans. She worked at Bailey's during most vacations, and Tessa had gotten to know her fairly well.

And Carly's reputation was stellar.

Bottom line: Tessa was overprotective when it came to Isabel, and that wasn't entirely a good thing.

She didn't want to be a helicopter parent.

On the other hand, with Marjory Laughlin in the world, she was afraid to take chances. Even sending Isabel to kindergarten and afternoon day care was still something of a challenge; Tessa's every instinct urged her to fuss and fret, ever watchful.

Therefore, if she couldn't find an appropriate sitter, she'd have to back out of her date with Jesse, skip the dance.

She'd feel like Cinderella if she had to do that—Cinderella with no prospect of a glass slipper and fairy godmother, never mind Prince Charming.

She gave up on her oatmeal and carried the bowl to the sink. She left the saucepan to soak and placed her uneaten breakfast in the refrigerator.

Isabel, whose thoughts had probably turned back to the adventure at Bitter Gulch, finished her food, placed her own bowl in the sink and hurried off to brush her teeth.

Once her daughter had finished in the bathroom, Tessa performed a few ablutions of her own. Checked her makeup—a light coat of mascara and some dark pink lip gloss—and pinned her hair up in a loose (messy?) bun.

Less than ten minutes later, she and her daughter—who skipped the whole way—reached the Methodist church where Isabel had kindergarten in the morning and day care in the afternoon.

"Have a good day, Isabel," Tessa told the child,

bending and speaking quietly. "And remember what we talked about. Be kind." She handed Isabel her bag lunch.

Isabel looked nonplussed by the reminder, which had probably been unnecessary, and turned away, about to scurry toward the cluster of children gathering at the front door under the supervision of an assistant.

Tessa hadn't let go of her daughter's hand, as expected, and Isabel turned to look back at her with some consternation wrinkling her little forehead.

"What, Mommy?" she asked, her tone just short of impatient.

"I love you, that's what," Tessa replied.

Isabel beamed, as if relieved. "I love you, too, Mommy!"

Tessa released the child's fingers, watched as she raced toward her best friend, Eleanor Susan Gwendolyn Gray.

"To the moon and back," Tessa whispered.

She waited, joined by several other moms, until the kids had been shepherded in through the church's side door.

An unexpected chill trickled down her back, like a drop of ice water, and she pulled her red coat closer around her.

She's safe here.

Isabel is safe, *in this building, with these people.*

Only mildly comforted, Tessa went back to the little rental house, where she spent the morning sweeping, dusting, making beds and doing laundry.

Just before noon, she heated up some canned soup and made a grilled cheese sandwich.

After lunch, she headed out, carefully locking the front door behind her.

She might just be the only person in Painted Pony Creek who locked her door, but so be it.

Tessa had good reason.

The walk to Vintage Treasures took almost fifteen minutes, and it served to ease her anxiety a little. That famous Big Sky was bluer than blue that day, and with nary a cloud. The air was fresh and chilly.

When Tessa reached the shop, she stopped on the sidewalk, taking in the items displayed in the front window.

A slightly dented tin dollhouse, very old. It was empty, but the walls and the floors marked it as probably a product of the 1950s—the '60s at the latest.

It was surrounded by a variety of other items— high-heeled shoes, handbags, gloves, a threadbare teddy bear.

Tessa's heart sank a little, but she soon recovered. It wasn't Christmas yet and, besides, she had a few things hidden away in the back of her closet—a stuffed pony from Walmart, clothes from a yard sale she'd gone to with Miranda over in Silver Hills, a child-size vanity table, complete with its own mirror and upholstered seat, from right here at Vintage Treasures. The vanity needed a paint job, but it was sturdy, and she knew Isabel would love it.

She was about to open the door and step inside the shop when she spotted the row of tiny dolls designed, obviously, to occupy a little house.

They looked to be carved out of wood, and, leaning in so close that her hair brushed the display window, Tessa took in their exquisitely painted faces, their tattered, old-fashioned clothes. They stood in a tidy row, mother, father, brother, sister.

Tessa was charmed.

A bell tinkled as she stepped into the shop, where the air was toasty warm and faintly musty—the smell of old things, long cherished.

Millie Collins, who had owned and operated the small shop for "donkey's years," as she put it, stepped out of the back room to greet Tessa. Her cap of silver-white hair gleamed in the dim light, and her blue eyes looked huge behind the lenses of her faux-tortoiseshell glasses.

"Tessa! I'm so glad to see you!" she said. Good-natured soul that she was, Millie was probably glad to see anybody and everybody, but Tessa allowed herself to be flattered anyway. "How can I help you?"

Tessa stood just inside the door, looking down at the dollhouse family. She was no master seamstress, but she could probably whip up a change of clothes for each of them.

It was easy to imagine the tiny crew peeking out of Isabel's stocking on Christmas morning.

"I'm actually looking for a dress," she said, probably sounding as distracted as she felt. "But these dolls have really caught my eye. How much for the set?"

"Fifteen dollars," Millie replied pleasantly, but with an underlying firmness that indicated she wouldn't be haggled with.

Not that Tessa ever haggled. She was half-again too proud for that—probably to her own disadvantage.

"They come from Germany," Millie went on. "Hand-crafted before the wars."

"They must have quite a history," Tessa replied, mentally counting the cash in her wallet, filched from the rainy-day money she kept stashed in a mason jar in her kitchen, behind the canned vegetables.

"I'm sure they do," Millie said. "But they're not haunted or anything like that."

"Haunted?" Tessa repeated, surprised.

"I know most people are skeptical about such things, but I had a marionette in here once—bought it at an estate sale up in Kalispell—and I swear that thing used to follow me with its painted-on eyes."

Tessa shivered. "Spooky," she said. "Did you sell it?"

"Heavens, no," Millie replied. "I tossed it in the burn-barrel and put a match to it. That thing gave me the creeps, and I didn't want to subject some innocent customer to that!"

Very gently, Tessa gathered up the tiny dolls from the display window and held them in a little bunch in one hand, like a delicate nosegay.

They were adorable.

And utterly benign.

She crossed to the counter, set them on the green felt blotter beside the antique cash register.

"I'll take them," she told Millie.

"I can throw in the dollhouse for another five dollars, since you're a regular customer," Millie offered.

Tessa shook her head, still admiring the dolls.

"My daughter and I will have a lot of fun constructing a home for them out of shoeboxes and the like," she said.

"How about the dress you mentioned? I have a red velvet number that would look swell on you." With that, Millie came out from behind the counter and crossed the shop to rummage through dresses dangling from brass hooks on the far wall. "If I remember right, it even has a few sequins."

She found the dress in question and brought it over for Tessa's inspection.

If she'd been a torch singer in a speakeasy, Tessa thought, as she examined the garish garment, it would have been perfect.

She rejected it politely and examined several others, at Millie's behest, finding none that fit both her taste and her budget.

She declined them all, paid for the German doll-house family and watched as Millie wrapped them in tissue paper.

Her old standby, the little black dress that was quite possibly in need of mending as well as dry cleaning, would have to do.

❄ 5 ❄

On impulse, and having plenty of time before Isabel got out of day care, Tessa stopped by Bailey's for a cup of coffee and a bowl of soup.

The place was doing a lively business, as usual, and people waved and called out greetings as she entered. Tessa responded with warm smiles and nods.

She hung her coat and purse from a hook inside the kitchen, feeling warm, inside and out.

There was one stool open at the long counter and she took it.

This was another perk of living in Painted Pony Creek; she felt welcome wherever she went: work, church, the shops, the post office, the supermarket. Here, it seemed folks were honestly glad to see each other.

There were, of course, miscreants of all degrees, gossips and other troublemakers, as there were in any community, but here, it seemed to Tessa, the good far outweighed the bad.

Carly Hollister appeared, smiling. She was a beautiful girl, with caramel-colored hair and pale amber eyes, and better still, she was genuinely friendly.

She produced a fresh bottle of hand sanitizer from under the counter, and Tessa pumped a few drops into one palm and rubbed her hands together.

"Thanks," she said. "Looks like you're having a busy day."

Carly laughed. "It's typical, as you know, between lunch and supper. What'll it be, Tessa?"

She ordered coffee and the soup of the day, chicken stew, as planned.

Carly served the coffee first, with the soup soon following. "Are you going to the big dance?" the girl asked. The crowd was thinning out a little, and Alice was busy at the cash register, while Miranda bused tables.

Day off or not, it was all Tessa could do not to forsake her coffee and soup and help out.

"Yes," Tessa replied. "Are you?"

Just then, the stool to Tessa's left opened, and Melba Summers slid into the space.

Both Tessa and Carly said hi to the chief. Then Carly replied to Tessa's question. "Nope," she said. "Eric can't make it back from school until the day before Thanksgiving, so I'll sit this one out."

Eric Worth was her longtime boyfriend.

"That's too bad."

"You're going?" Carly asked, smiling and leaning in a little. "With whom, if I may ask?"

Tessa blushed. "Jesse McKettrick."

"Can't say I didn't see *that* coming," Melba put in.

"I might have to back out," Tessa confessed. She hadn't meant to give voice to the thought; it had just slipped out.

"Why?" chorused Melba and Carly.

"It might be hard to find a babysitter," Tessa replied, wishing she'd kept her mouth shut. "I was thinking of asking Hayley Worth, but I'm sure she has a date for the dance. She's so popular."

"Problem solved," Carly said breezily. "I can babysit for you." She stretched her neck to look around the restaurant, made sure she wasn't needed. Bailey's was in between rushes, though, and all but empty. Once she was sure things were under control amid the tables and booths, she added, "Isabel knows me, remember. We color pictures together on my breaks sometimes."

That was true. Isabel usually arrived from day care a few minutes after three, and on days when Tessa was needed for an extra hour or so, Carly, Miranda and Alice did their best to keep the child entertained.

"Seriously?" Tessa asked. "My car isn't running at the moment. I couldn't pick you up *or* take you home after the dance."

Carly made a face. "I have a car," she said. "Any other problems?"

"No," Tessa lied, thrown off by how easily the baby-sitting dilemma had been solved.

"What are you going to wear?" Melba asked. She was studying the menu—and missing nothing of the conversation.

"I have this black cocktail dress—"

"Doesn't sound very festive," Melba remarked after ordering the same late lunch Tessa had—coffee and soup. "You ought to wear red," she added when Tessa didn't respond. "'Tis almost the season, after all. And you look fantastic in red."

It *was* Tessa's best color, and one of her favorites. "I looked at a crimson number at Vintage Treasures," she murmured, unable to disguise her disappointment. "It didn't suit me, and it probably wasn't my size anyhow."

By then, Miranda had joined the confab, stepping

up alongside Carly. "You know I sew," she said. "I could have altered the dress to fit you like the proverbial glove!"

Ruefully, Tessa shook her head. "It was too gaudy," she said, "and the neckline would come almost to my navel."

Laughter all around.

Tessa remembered the dollhouse family and brightened. "I found something marvelous for Isabel, though." With that, she jumped up, went to her purse, still on the hook just inside the kitchen, and carefully pulled out the four tiny toys, so carefully wrapped in tissue paper.

She returned to her stool, set the small packet on the countertop, displacing her soup bowl to do so, and undid the wrapping to reveal the dolls.

"My, my," said Alice, peering over her shoulder. "Those are marvelous!"

"I've never seen anything like them," Carly said, sounding a little bewitched.

"They need new outfits, and I'm just the woman to make them," said Miranda. Everyone knew she was a skilled potter—she probably earned more from selling her work through local gift shops than she did putting in eight hours at Bailey's—but it was news to Tessa that Miranda could sew well enough to alter vamp dresses and clothe dolls. "I have *tons* of fabric scraps at home, left over from quilting and some of my textile pieces."

Before anyone could respond, she rummaged through her own purse—stashed on a shelf under the counter— and produced a measuring tape, a small notebook and a pen.

"You'd do that?" Tessa asked. Would she never get used to the generosity of this town? These people?

"Sure," said Miranda. "I love Isabel. She's a great kid."

"But—well…" Tessa stumbled verbally, blushed. "How much would you charge?"

"Charge? This is going to be *fun*," Miranda replied. Finished taking measurements and making notes, she put everything back into her purse. "No charge."

"I've got a red dress that would look great on you," Melba put in eagerly. "It's Dan's favorite, and I wear it whenever I want to remind him why we have three kids and how we got them."

Everyone laughed again, including Tessa.

Then she had another rickety moment. "You were probably planning to wear it to the Thanksgiving dance yourself, then," she said.

Melba grinned. "Not me," she replied immediately. "Three kids are *plenty*. Besides, I have to work that night." She looked Tessa over with frank dispatch. "I think it would fit you well enough. Might be a little too long, since I'm taller than you are, but that's just a matter of raising the hemline."

"Melba, I couldn't ask you to—"

"You *didn't* ask me," Melba interrupted kindly. "If you're free tonight, I'll bring the dress over to your place, and you can try it on."

"I'll come, too," Miranda said, inviting herself. "I can put in a hem and take a few tucks here and there—" She paused, glanced Melba's way, as if fearing she'd offended her, and seeing that she hadn't, she went on. "If that's okay with you, Tessa. I shouldn't have invited myself."

"Of course you're both welcome, but—"

"But nothing," Melba interjected. "I get off at six today. I can swing by between seven and seven thirty and pick Miranda up on my way over."

Tessa's head was spinning a little.

In that moment, she was finally able to picture herself staying here in Painted Pony Creek for good, without any of her previous misgivings. Settling down with Isabel and making a simple but secure life for the both of them.

"You're all so kind," she began, and promptly faltered. She very nearly burst into tears, not only because she'd never had friends like these in her life, but also because she knew Marjory Laughlin was out there, biding her time, circling slowly, like a shark.

When she struck, there would be bloodshed.

Looking directly into Tessa's probably pale face, Melba drew in a sharp breath. "Why, you look like death, all of a sudden. What on earth is the matter?"

She couldn't tell them.

She'd asked local authorities for help in the past, only to be told there was nothing law enforcement could do unless Marjory made an aggressive move.

The whole thing was, in the police's view, a "domestic matter," outside their jurisdiction.

Sure, Melba was different, a truly caring friend, but the law was still the law.

"I think—I think I'm getting a headache," Tessa said.

It wasn't a lie. Thoughts of Brent's stepmother always affected her this way.

Her earlier determination to stay in Painted Pony Creek wavered slightly, as she was suddenly awash in self-doubt. Had she been deluding herself when she'd vowed to stop running and have it out with Marjory once and for all?

Did she even have a choice?

Her car still wasn't running and, as far as she was concerned, that made her a sitting duck.

Yes, Marjory had been quiet for a while, but that wasn't necessarily a good sign. She was perfectly capable of lying low, keeping her distance while Tessa settled into a cozy, happy, *safe* life with Isabel, here in Dreamtown, USA.

"That must be some headache," Alice observed, frowning a little. "Would you like to go upstairs to the apartment and rest awhile?"

Tessa shook her head, got off the stool.

The headache was getting worse.

The neon lights in the jukebox were too bright, and the long fluorescent bulbs overhead buzzed.

She resisted an urge to put her hands over her ears and squeeze her eyes shut, but that would only make Carly, Alice, Miranda and Melba worry more.

"I'll be all right," she said. "Really. I just need to take some aspirin, maybe lie down for half an hour."

The other women were all frowning.

"I'll drive you home," Melba stated firmly. "And I'll pick Isabel up at day care—what time does she get out?"

Tessa shook her head. Her stomach threatened to rebel against the chicken stew she'd just eaten and send it flying. "They have strict orders not to release Isabel to anyone but me," she managed to say.

"I *am* the chief of police," Melba pointed out. "You can call them and say it's all right to release Isabel to me *or* you and I can just stop by the church and pick her up now."

Tessa nodded. "Let's do that," she murmured, wildly grateful for such help and concern. "Pick her up together, I mean."

Five minutes later, Tessa and Melba entered the day care center by a side door and collected Isabel.

The little girl took one look at her mother's face and said, "You look sick, Mommy. Do you have a temperature?"

Tessa smiled through the pounding headache and the blood thundering in her ears. "No, honey," she said. "I just need to rest for a little while."

Isabel seemed skeptical. "You *always* say that," she accused, but with concern. "I get scared when you're sick."

Tessa pulled the child against her side, gave her a one-armed hug. "Don't be. I'm fine. Just—*tired*."

Isabel spotted Melba's official SUV by the curb and her eyes lit up. "Do we get to ride in your car again, Mrs. Chief?" she asked with delight.

"You sure do," Melba replied, with a chuckle. "I've even got a booster seat for you. I took my little boy, Danny, to the doctor this morning, and he needs one just like you do."

Melba helped Isabel into the safety seat in back while Tessa groped for the door handle on the front passenger side, hoping she wouldn't throw up as soon as the wheels started turning.

Fortunately, she didn't.

They made it all the way to her place, up the front walk and through the entrance before she had to make a bumbling run for the bathroom.

An hour later, bundled up in a warm blanket and nestled on the couch, with its broken springs and faint smell of tobacco smoke, Tessa felt better.

Melba had brewed her a cup of tea and made sure Isabel was okay before leaving. After determining that Tessa was still up for trying on a dress, she'd gone back to work.

Isabel, meanwhile, had stayed close, worried.

Tessa was rarely sick, and when she was, she went to great lengths to hide it from her daughter.

This time, there had been no skirting the ugly truth.

"Maybe you have a brain tumor," Isabel said, speculating. "I saw a movie, over at Eleanor Susan Gwendolyn

Gray's house, about a woman who had one of those."
She paused, swallowed. "She died."

"That doesn't sound like the kind of movie you
should be watching." Making a mental note to confer
with the other little girl's mother about media content,
Tessa reached out, found her daughter's hand, squeezed
it. "I'm definitely not going to die, sweetheart. Not
until a long, long and even longer time from now."

"You promise?"

"I promise," Tessa said, hoping she hadn't just committed a mortal sin.

"You need to go to a doctor," Isabel stated impla-
cably.

Oddly enough, Tessa thought of Jesse's remark, the
night before, when he'd kissed her and she'd spouted
off like an idiot about not being on birth control.

Two birds, one stone, she thought. Though she'd never
in her life even consider hurting a bird.

There was a community clinic in the Creek, two
doors down from the Methodist church. Tessa would
go there, since she didn't have health insurance, have
her head examined and pick up a prescription.

The thought of the latter must have brought color
back to her face, because Isabel beamed at her.

"You're feeling better!" she said.

"I am," Tessa replied.

By the time Miranda and Melba showed up, Melba carrying a garment bag and Miranda a sewing kit, Tessa was very nearly her old self.

She'd had a moment of weakness, when it had seemed she had no choice but to run away again, but a warm shower, a bouquet of pinkish-white roses from Jesse and a light supper had made her braver than before. More hopeful.

Miranda zeroed right in on the spill of luscious rose-buds, not even stopping to take off her coat. They were on display in the center of the coffee table.

"These are spectacular!" the older woman observed with a broad smile.

"Mr. McKettrick sent them," Isabel informed them all. "I think he likes Mommy."

"Seems like a good bet," said Melba, taking off her uniform jacket to reveal her customary shirt and slacks. Her smile, directed at Tessa, was a little on the saucy side.

Miranda began, mischievously, to hum "Here Comes the Bride."

Tessa laughed, even as a corner of her heart went aquiver at the thought of being an actual bride. More specifically, *Jesse McKettrick's* bride.

"Stop it," she said. "Does anyone want tea? Or coffee?"

"Nothing for me," Melba said, opening the garment bag to reveal a shimmery swath of deep red fabric. "My mom has the kids tonight and Dan's making a special for dinner for just the two of us."

"Here we go again," Miranda teased. "That gleam in your eye says it all, Melba Summers. I bet you'll be expecting number four by Christmas!"

Melba gave a pretended glare.

Miranda laughed.

An image of Melba's husband, Dan, crossed Tessa's mind. He was a big man—football player–type big— and he was handsome. He had run an international security firm for years, and before that, he'd been both a navy SEAL and an FBI agent. Melba, too, had been an FBI agent.

These days Dan seemed to be a househusband, since he had so much free time. He and Melba had quite a history—they'd been married, divorced and then *re*-married—and Tessa was curious about their love story, though she'd never pried.

It was just plain none of her business.

Period.

The next hour passed in a hurry.

Tessa tried on the dress—it was an amazing garment, exquisitely cut and probably tailor-made for Melba's sleek, very fit body—and it was several inches too long, as predicted, since Melba was taller. The bodice was loose, too, which prompted a round of silly remarks and giggles suited to a younger crowd.

Isabel, by that time, had been put to bed.

Between bouts of laughter, Miranda had measured and tucked and pinned, muttering to herself.

When she'd finished, Melba stood back and let out a low whistle of exclamation. "*Damn*, girl, you do look sizzling hot in that dress!"

Not wanting to be poked by any of the many pins Miranda had put in place, Tessa did a sort of shuffling walk to the bathroom, where she stood looking at herself in the time-spotted mirror on the back of the door.

Melba and Miranda squeezed in behind her, making the whole evening seem even more like a teenage slumber party than it already had.

Tessa, in the meantime, was flabbergasted by the transformation from jeans-clad mommy to *hey, there, cowboy* babe-on-the-prowl.

The rich red and soft shine of the silken fabric made for a powerful combo.

Tessa opened her mouth, discovered she had nothing to say and closed it again.

Melba and Miranda, for their part, had *plenty* to say.

"You'll need to wear red lipstick, of course," Miranda said.

"And pin your hair up in a loose bun, with plenty of little curly tendrils falling around your face," Melba put in.

Tessa, princess for a minute, came back down to Earth with a thud. Suddenly, she felt panicked, out of her depth and, somehow, shamelessly presumptuous.

"I can't possibly wear this dress!" she exclaimed in a ragged whisper. "What if it gets torn, or stained? And won't the alterations have a permanent effect on the fabric?" She turned, faced her two friends. "Oh, Melba, if I ruined your dress somehow, after all your kindness, I'd just die!"

"It's a *dress*," Melba stated emphatically. "And if you don't wear it to the Thanksgiving dance, I'm going to be insulted."

Tessa short-stepped it out of the bathroom, and Melba and Miranda trailed after her.

In the living room, she suddenly began to cry.

Melba steered her to a chair, and then she and Miranda sat down on the couch, hands folded in their laps.

"All right," Melba said. "Spill it, Tessa. Why the tears? What's going on?"

"And don't say you're just tired," Miranda added.

"Talk to us," Melba reiterated, sounding gentle and stern, both at once. "We're not leaving until we get an answer."

"Help me out of this dress first," Tessa said. "There's a pin sticking me in the backside and I don't want to cry all over this lovely silk."

Once she was back in her jeans and T-shirt, Tessa sat down and said, "You're not going to let me out of this, are you?" She felt both defeated and oddly relieved.

"No," replied Melba. "We've all known, since you first arrived, that you were on the lam from somebody or some*thing*. We've been patient, Tessa. Nobody wanted to get all up in your personal business, but today you were actually *sick* with some secret you're keeping, and I, for one, am done waiting."

"You have to promise not to tell anyone else," Tessa ventured hesitantly.

"If the law is involved," Melba said, "I can't make that promise. I took an oath."

"I think I can promise," Miranda volunteered, albeit uncertainly.

Tessa straightened her spine, lifted her chin and told

them all about her brief relationship with Brent Laughlin and its ending, about her pregnancy and the trust fund for Isabel's education and Marjory's crazy campaign to take Isabel away.

"Holy crap," said Miranda when the story finally fizzled to an end.

"That's a whole *other* kind of crap," pronounced Melba, slapping her lean, muscular thighs with the palms of both hands. "This Marjory woman is crazy. She has no legal or moral right to your child."

The conversation was sotto voce, since no one wanted Isabel to overhear.

"That doesn't seem to matter to Marjory," Tessa pointed out. "She still believes she has a case against me—raising a child while poor, or something. I think her plan is to make me look bad, bad enough that some judge will take her side." She looked frantically from one concerned face to the other. "And she has the kind of money to *buy* a judge or two, if she hasn't already. Plus, I'm afraid she might resort to kidnapping—she tried that once and failed, thank God, though just barely. Again, she's rich. If she snatches Isabel—" she paused, closed her eyes, shuddered "—and takes her out of the country, I might never see my baby again."

"Have you heard from her?" Melba asked crisply,

clearly back on the job. "Recently, I mean? Does she know where you are?"

"I haven't heard from her directly," Tessa replied. "But as to whether or not she knows Isabel and I are here in Painted Pony Creek, well, it's hard to say. She has so many resources—she can reach in all directions, like tree roots."

"Three things," Melba said, lifting the corresponding number of fingers on her right hand. "Number one, you need a lawyer. This woman is harassing you, Tessa, and that's against the law. Number two, we—you and I—need to let Sheriff Garrett know about this. His people and mine will keep a close watch on you, and especially Isabel. Number three, I'm going to ask my husband to check Marjory Laughlin *and* her stepson out online. Dan's a security expert—the best there is, in my biased opinion."

Tessa was overwhelmed and chagrined. "No offense, Melba, but the police haven't been much help in the past. They pretty much brushed me off as a disgruntled ex-girlfriend trying to make trouble for a pillar of the community."

"Well, things are different here," Melba said. "Eli Garrett and I take our duty seriously. And *our duty* is to the people of this county and this town, whether they're settling here or just passing through."

Tessa sighed. "I'm so tired of running," she said. "And I know it isn't good for Isabel. She's made friends here, both at Bailey's and at school, and she'll be devastated if we have to hit the road again." She paused. "Not that we could, with my car broken down. There's always the bus, but we'd have to leave most of our belongings behind and, besides, buses move so slowly— it would be all too easy for Marjory or her people to track the schedules and find out exactly where we were headed."

Miranda reached over to pat Tessa's hand in a sweet, motherly fashion. "Do you want me to spend the night, honey? I could sleep on the couch and—" she glanced Melba's way, very briefly, before focusing on Tessa again "—and I'm licensed to carry. There's a .38 in my purse."

Melba turned a thunderous gaze on Miranda. "Say *what*?" she demanded. "There's a *child* in this house, woman!"

Miranda straightened her spine and her face took on a slightly stubborn expression. "You can't arrest me, Melba Summers. Like I said, I'm *licensed*."

"You're also crazy," Melba retorted. "Are you actually telling me that you've been sashaying around this town with a *gun* in your handbag?"

"You didn't think I was crazy when I stopped those nasty men who tried to rob the drugstore while I was waiting for my prescriptions four years ago," Miranda replied, giving as good as she got. "I held those two ya-hoos until you and Eli came and took over. You were just a deputy then, of course."

This last line was delivered with a faintly smug note.

Tessa was gobsmacked.

Miranda, sweet, blunt Miranda, had been *packing* all this time?

At Bailey's. In the supermarket. Maybe even in church.

The idea was terrifying—and slightly reassuring, too.

"*Damn* it," Melba barked, though she kept her voice low for Isabel's sake, "this isn't the Old West!"

"I never said it was," Miranda answered, pursing her lips a little.

"Ladies," Tessa interrupted, putting up both hands, palms out, in a gesture of peace. "We're off-topic here, don't you think?"

She wasn't particularly keen on the idea of resuming the Marjory discussion, but the tension between these two women was getting to her.

"This argument isn't over," Melba informed Miranda tersely.

"Whatever you say, Chief," Miranda replied, apparently undaunted.

Melba stood. "We'd better be going," she said. She was speaking more moderately now, but at a price, Tessa knew.

"I'll have this ready in a day or two," Miranda said, gathering the red dress from the back of a chair, where Tessa had placed it after changing back into her regular clothes. With brisk motions, the older woman put it carefully back into its garment bag.

"If you hear anything from this Marjory person," Melba told Tessa, ignoring Miranda, at least for the moment, "call me immediately." She paused, frowned. "You do have a cell phone, don't you?"

"Yes," Tessa replied. "I do."

Melba took out her own phone—which was state-of-the-art. "Let's have your number," she said, clearly in cop mode.

Tessa recited her number. Her own phone was refurbished, and certainly not the latest version, but it worked fine.

After goodbyes and thank-yous from Tessa, Melba and Miranda took their leave.

Tessa saw them to the door, waved as they drove away and finally locked up.

She spent several minutes tidying the living room, then retrieved her phone from her purse, planning to enter Melba's number and put the device on the charger.

She forgot to do it sometimes, and that always made her feel uneasy.

There was a text waiting, a reply to one she'd sent earlier, thanking Jesse for the roses.

You're welcome was his reply.

Tessa bit her lower lip, considering.

She typed **Any chance you could come by tonight?**

Immediately, she backspaced, erasing the question.

Hey, she wrote instead. **What are you up to?**

She hesitated, finger poised over the send button.

It was closing in on nine o'clock, and Jesse worked in construction. He might be in bed already.

The thought of Jesse in bed made a muscle leap in the pit of her stomach.

Did he sleep naked? Wear sweatpants or boxers?

Stop, she commanded herself silently.

Her gaze fell on the packet Isabel had taken from the mailbox with such exuberance the day before and intuitively Tessa knew why she hadn't opened it yet.

She tapped Send, mostly by accident as she reached for the oversize brown envelope.

She turned it over, looking for a return address.

There wasn't one, but the postmark was identification enough all by itself.

Boston, MA.

The phone rang in Tessa's hand, causing her to start.

Squeezing her eyes shut while she drew a deep breath, she answered with an awkward "Er, hello?"

"It's Jesse," came the reply. "I wanted to hear your voice, so I called instead of texting. Hope that's okay."

Tessa opened her eyes, took another deep breath, and then another. "Jesse." That was all she said. Just his name.

"What's wrong?" he asked.

Obviously, she'd given herself away—maybe it was something in her tone of voice—and there was no point in trying to convince him otherwise.

"A lot, actually," she replied. "Listen, Jesse, I don't want to be that person—the one who asks for legal advice outside office hours, but—"

"Tessa, what's going on?"

"Can you come over? I'd rather talk face-to-face." She swallowed hard. "I know it's kind of late, so I'll understand if you say no."

"I'll be there in twenty minutes," Jesse responded.
"Mind if I bring my dog? He's been alone all day, so
I'd hate to leave him again."

Strangely, Tessa's eyes brimmed with tears.

Also strangely, she laughed.

"Sure," she said. "Bring the dog."

❄ 6 ❄

With Norvel riding shotgun, Jesse headed for town in his truck.

As he pulled up to Tessa's place, she stepped out onto the porch.

The light from inside rimmed her like an aura.

Norvel, always up for meeting new people, gave a happy little yip and tried to squeeze between Jesse and the steering wheel so he could jump out the moment the door opened.

Gently, Jesse eased the dog back into the other seat.

"Wait here for a minute," he said.

Norvel, who understood English even if he couldn't speak it, whimpered once and settled into the passenger seat again. His tongue lolled.

"You can't go charging people, bud," Jesse went on, and never mind that he was reasoning with man's best friend, not another person. "Give the lady a chance to decide whether she wants a face-full of dog, okay?"

Norvel whimpered again, but he relaxed a little.

Carefully, Jesse opened the driver's-side door. "Stay," he reiterated.

Norvel was sitting tight, though he practically buzzed with delight.

Jesse glanced at Tessa again and admitted to himself that he was as eager to be near her as his dog was.

He got out of the truck, shut the door quickly.

Norvel, well-trained critter that he was, remained in the passenger seat.

Tessa met Jesse on the sidewalk, looked past him at Norvel and managed a shaky little smile.

"Is he friendly?" she asked so quietly that Jesse had to lean in to hear her. Not that he minded leaning in. *Hell* no. She smelled faintly of lavender and fresh air.

"Yes," Jesse answered, surprised by the steadiness in his own voice.

Tessa was scared; he'd heard it in her voice over the phone, and now he saw it in her face.

"I think I'm in trouble," she said simply, confirming his concern.

The pit of Jesse's stomach dipped a little. "Okay, let's go inside and talk about it."

"Your dog can come in, too," she added, though she'd already turned away from Jesse and started back up the front walk.

Jesse clipped a leash to Norvel's collar in case he got overenthusiastic and followed Tessa.

The suspense was killing him as she closed the door and took his coat.

What *kind* of trouble was she in?

Was she a fugitive? A battered wife? The sole witness to a federal crime?

All those possibilities, plus a few more, came to Jesse's mind as he waited for an explanation.

Tessa retrieved a manila envelope from a side table, handed it to him and sat down in an armchair that dwarfed her.

Norvel, meanwhile, curled up at Jesse's feet, muzzle resting on his forelegs, rolling his mismatched eyes from one human to the other.

Jesse shoved a hand through his hair. He'd showered after he'd finished work and the chores out at Liam's place, but he wasn't sure if he'd bothered with a comb.

He'd been wearing boxers and nothing else when he'd called Tessa, and he'd dressed in haste. Never bothered to check himself out in a mirror. He hoped he looked presentable.

He glanced down at the envelope.

"Before you open that," Tessa said quietly, "I need to tell you that I can't pay you. Not up front, at least. We can probably work out a payment plan, if you're willing."

Jesse shook his head. "These days, my work is ninety percent pro bono. There won't be a bill, Tessa."

"I'm not sure I'm comfortable with that," she replied, sweetly earnest and more than a little embarrassed if her expression was anything to go by. "But I need your help, so maybe we can argue the point later."

Jesse lifted the envelope slightly. "May I? Or would you rather explain in advance?"

Her lush mouth tightened slightly, softened again. "It's largely self-explanatory, I think," she answered in her own good time. "But of course I'll answer any questions you have afterward."

He pulled the thin sheaf of papers from the envelope, which he set aside.

The first thing he noticed was a check, neatly paper-clipped to the document, in the amount of $100,000. It was made out to Tessa.

He looked up at her, saw that she'd gone pale, and

repressed an urge to take her hand and pull her from her chair to sit beside him on the couch.

Or, better yet, on his lap.

Jesse lifted the check, scanned the document beneath.

It was several pages long and written in legalese, which didn't surprise him.

When he reached the end, he went back to the beginning and read the whole thing again, slowly.

Essentially, the document stated that Tessa was being asked to surrender her child to one Marjory Laughlin. There was no signature line, no space for a notary stamp; the check itself, according to the weird contract, constituted agreement on Tessa's part if she cashed it.

The thing might have been dictated to someone, but it hadn't been composed by an attorney.

"This is all kinds of wrong," Jesse said. "The woman is basically trying to *buy* your daughter."

Paler than before, Tessa nodded.

"She can be sued for this, Tessa. Possibly even arrested for attempting to traffic another human being." He paused, thrust his hand through his hair again, this time in frustration. At his feet, Norvel lifted his head and perked up his floppy ears. "Who *is* this person, anyhow?"

Very slowly, and with no little reluctance, Tessa told him the story.

Marjory, she explained, was her ex's stepmother, a very wealthy widow with connections up the wazoo. Tessa had never intended to sign the check, but she was frightened just the same. Marjory had legally adopted Brent in his teens, which meant she saw herself as Isabel's rightful grandmother. And she was obsessed with taking control of her heir's child. She wasn't above taking drastic action in order to get her way.

And that, evidently, included kidnapping.

"Have you discussed this with Chief Summers or Sheriff Garrett?" he asked.

Tessa picked at the threadbare upholstery on her armchair. "Melba knows—about Marjory and Brent, anyway. I told her and Miranda all about them earlier, when they stopped by to—well, when they stopped by. But I hadn't opened the envelope yet."

"And what advice did the chief give you?"

"She said I needed a lawyer, and she made it sound pretty urgent, so after I'd read the document, I texted you. She wants me to let Sheriff Garrett know and she's asking her husband, Dan, to look into the situation online."

"Have you spoken to Brent? Asked him to rein in his crazy stepmother?"

Tessa shook her head. "Even if he wanted to help, I don't think he could do anything to stop her from harassing Isabel and me. He's a total mama's boy. I get the feeling Marjory got him to rely on her for all things financial when he was a kid, and he never broke the habit. Even though he's heir to the kingdom, Marjory has a certain amount of control over his financial dealings."

Jesse went still, pondering a course of action.

Tessa waited in nervous silence for a long while, then blurted, "I'm so sorry, Jesse. I have no business dragging you into this mess. We hardly know each other."

"You're not dragging me into anything, Tessa. I want to help. So will Eli Garrett once he hears about this."

Tessa still seemed at least partially unconvinced. "I've gone to the police before," she told him. "In three different states. Every time, I was told nothing could be done, because it was a 'family' issue." Color surged beneath Tessa's beautiful cheekbones, pulsed there. "In other words, unless Marjory did us bodily harm, or actually stole my child, I was out of luck."

"She's been harassing you, plain and simple. *Stalking* you. Let's just say, not all cops are like Eli and the chief. In fact, *most* law enforcement officers are dedicated people. I'll go to the sheriff's office with you tomorrow, and you can file a complaint—*and* apply for a restraining order. If Ms. Laughlin violates that, she'll be in handcuffs before she knows what hit her."

Tessa looked just slightly hopeful.

Jesse, being a lawyer, was still in question mode. "Has she approached you in person? Have you seen her—or anyone else—following you around, or maybe just watching you? Has she called, sent you emails or texts?"

"I thought I saw her once, months ago, before we came here," Tessa said. "I was working in a diner, and a stretch limo pulled up outside. The windows were tinted, and no one came inside or even got out of the car, but Marjory is a platinum blonde, and I was sure I caught sight of her hair. It's quite distinctive."

Jesse had picked up a pen from the coffee table, and he was making notes on the back of the manila envelope.

"I've had a few texts, too," Tessa added. "Every time I changed my cell phone number, Marjory knew what it was."

"Did you screenshot them?" Jesse asked.

Tessa nodded, swallowed visibly. "I've documented everything I could."

"That's good. Do you have contact information for her or her stepson?"

Tessa actually shuddered. "Not the personal kind, but Brent at least shouldn't be hard to reach. He works for the family corporation in Boston, or he did when I left. His stepmother isn't actively involved in the business, as far as I know, but she's a control freak for sure, so she probably hangs around a lot."

"Okay," Jesse said, clicking the pen once and then laying it back down on the coffee table. "For tonight, that's all I need."

Tessa let out a long, quivering sigh. "Thank you," she said. "For coming here, for everything."

Jesse acknowledged her words, but he probably sounded distracted, since he was frowning and looking around him.

"How safe is this place, Tessa? Do you have an alarm system? Security cameras?"

"No," Tessa said. "I don't think the owners are into technology. When I moved in, there was one of those heavy black telephones installed—the kind you have to dial. The Farridays took it away with them after we did a walk-through and I agreed to rent the place."

"No lease?" Jesse asked.

"No lease," Tessa confirmed. "I always rent month to month, just in case."

"Just in case you have to leave on a moment's notice?"

"That's about it," she admitted. "Thing is, I'm tired of running, Jesse. It's too hard on Isabel." She paused, eyeing him. "And it's hard for me, too."

"If you've decided to dig in and stand your ground," Jesse offered quietly, "you couldn't have picked a better place than Painted Pony Creek."

"I'm beginning to realize that," Tessa replied thoughtfully. "I hate to even *think* about going away."

Jesse felt a bit of guilt for not telling Tessa he planned on leaving town after Bitter Gulch was up and running and Liam and the kids had moved into the main house, out on the ranch.

The thought that Tessa might not change her mind about leaving the Creek, should anything serious develop between the two of them, niggled at the back of Jesse's mind.

He decided to worry about that later.

As things stood, he'd taken Tessa on a single date, and an unorthodox one at that, and kissed her exactly twice. And, yes, she'd agreed to go to the Thanksgiving dance with him, but those things didn't add up to a relationship.

He was attracted to Tessa—*very* attracted—but any single man in his right mind would have been, would have wanted to get to know her, spend time with her. She was beautiful, in a simple, wholesome way that made Jesse ache inside, and she was brave, even though she probably didn't think so.

And right up there with her other charms was her do-or-die commitment to her child.

Tessa Stafford was the kind of mother, in fact, that he wanted for his own children, should he be lucky enough to have any.

"I don't think you and Isabel should be alone until the situation with Marjory Laughlin is resolved," he said.

Tessa's expressive brown eyes widened. "We don't have much choice," she said hesitantly.

Jesse patted the ratty sofa. "Let me spend the night," he said. "Or pack a bag and bundle Isabel up, and we'll head for my place."

Her eyes widened even farther and her mouth dropped open, though she quickly closed it. Pressed her lips together for a moment.

Jesse reached over, took her hand, though very lightly.

"Listen, Tess," he said, not planning until he'd said it to shorten her name, to reveal the affection he felt for her. "I'm not going to push myself on you. I just want to make sure you're safe."

"I've looked after myself—and Isabel—for a long time, Jesse," she pointed out.

He couldn't read her tone—or her expression.

"I know that," Jesse replied. "And I'm not suggesting anything permanent, but until we're sure the Wicked Witch isn't going to pop out of the woodwork and hurt you, or grab Isabel and run, I think we need to be extra careful." He let go of her fingers and dropped his hands between his knees. Norvel had lost interest in the conversation and fallen asleep, snoring a little.

Tessa said nothing.

Jesse met and held her gaze. "If you're uncomfortable, well, I'm not the only option. There are half a dozen families in the Creek—probably more—who would gladly let you and Isabel stay with them for a while."

Still without speaking, Tessa walked out of the room, returning presently with sheets, blankets and a pillow.

She set them in the armchair, and she and Jesse folded down the tattered and visibly lumpy couch. There was a deep crevice in the middle, which would make sleeping a challenge, but he didn't mind.

For tonight, he could protect Tessa and Isabel, and that was enough.

He awoke the next morning feeling ill-rested, scruffy and a little disoriented.

"Hello," Isabel stated, standing beside the couch. "I think your dog needs to go outside."

Norvel's furry mug appeared alongside Isabel's shining face.

Jesse yawned big and stretched, glad he'd slept in his clothes, since he'd thrown off the covers and even the top sheet.

"Right," he said and, swinging his legs over the side of the couch, he reached for his boots and pulled them on.

"How come you stayed overnight?" Isabel inquired cheerfully, one hand resting companionably on top of Norvel's head. "Did you and Mommy have a slumber party?"

Tessa appeared in the kitchen doorway, arms folded, leaning a shoulder against the frame. A little grin quirked at the corner of her mouth.

"We were talking business," she told her daughter. "No slumber party."

Jesse grinned at Tessa, rose to his feet. "Not this time, anyhow," he said.

Tessa blushed.

Jesse found the leash, hooked it to Norvel's collar, borrowed a wad of paper towels and took the dog out. Fortunately, Tessa's garbage cans were easy to find.

He was shivering when he came back into the house.

"Coffee's ready," Tessa said.

Jesse made for the bathroom, washed his hands, splashed his face with lukewarm water and studied himself in the medicine cabinet mirror above the sink.

He looked as though he'd just come from an all-night poker game, with his hair all rumpled—it was getting shaggy and he probably needed a trim—and his beard growing in. He rubbed his chin thoughtfully, wondering what Tessa saw when she looked at him.

He wasn't about to ask.

Returning to the kitchen, he accepted a mug of black coffee from Tessa—high-octane this time, instead of decaf. Which was a relief, since he felt like five miles of bad road.

"Did you sleep well?" she asked, setting a cast-iron skillet on the gas stove and bending to check the flame.

"No," Jesse answered.

She laughed. Took a package of bacon and a carton of eggs from the fridge.

Jesse's mouth watered. Since this was a household

of women, he'd half expected yogurt and a banana, if anything.

"At least you're honest," she said.

The statement caused Jesse a pang of guilt.

Tessa had practically told him her life story the night before, while he'd revealed a little about his family, particularly Liam, mentioned the ranch—strictly superficial stuff.

At some point, he'd have to tell her about Cynthia, and his former best friend, and the little boy who should have been his.

She needed to know, too, that, much as he liked Painted Pony Creek, he meant to move on.

It was too early for any of that, of course, but Jesse was concerned just the same.

Breakfast was excellent, like Tessa's coffee, and once they'd eaten, he insisted on cleaning up.

Tessa left the room to help Isabel get ready for another day. Because the house was so small, Jesse could hear them chatting happily away in Isabel's room, though he didn't pick up on the words, didn't try.

He just liked the sound.

And he liked not being alone.

That being the weekend, the courthouse was closed and there was no kindergarten or day care for Isabel.

Tessa took the day off and planned to spend it cleaning. Jesse had a better idea.

"You've seen Bitter Gulch," he said when mother and daughter reentered the kitchen. "How about a visit to my brother's ranch?"

A visible jolt of excitement went through Isabel's tiny frame, and it struck Jesse as unaccountably poignant. Even made the backs of his eyes burn.

"Are there horses?" she asked, practically jumping up and down by then.

"A couple," Jesse replied, glancing at Tessa as he spoke, and his voice sounded hoarse in his own ears. "A gelding—he's mine—and a Shetland that belongs to my niece and nephew."

"What's a Shetland?" Isabel wanted to know.

"A Shetland is a pony," Tessa explained.

Isabel's eyes were the size of saucers. "A *pony*? Like a really little horse?"

"Yes," Jesse said with a smile. He was trying to read Tessa's expression, figure out if he'd effed up somehow.

He should have discussed the whole idea of a visit to the ranch with Tessa before mentioning it in front of Isabel.

"Can I ride the pony?" Isabel asked with such hope that Jesse's throat tightened briefly.

"That's up to your mom," Jesse said, then mouthed *Sorry* to Tessa.

"We'll see," Tessa said.

"Can I pet it?" Isabel persisted. "Even if you won't let me ride the pony, can I pet it?"

Tessa's sudden, sun-coming-out-from-behind-the-clouds smile was a relief to Jesse, and probably to Isabel as well.

Young as she was, that kid didn't miss much.

"How about it, Tessa?" Jesse asked quietly. "It's a great place, the ranch, and I'd really like to show you around."

Tessa looked at her daughter, then back at Jesse. "Okay," she said. "It would be nice to have a change of scene, I think."

Fifteen minutes later, they were all in Jesse's truck, Norvel included, headed for the ranch.

Once they passed the town limits, the countryside was wide-open, and Tessa, gorgeous in that red coat of hers—*damn*, she looked good in red—seemed happy to undertake this ordinary adventure.

Glancing at her now and then as he navigated country roads, Jesse felt another shift, deep inside.

Tessa had faced so many challenges—she faced them still—struggling to care for and protect her child, rattling from town to town and state to state in that old wreck of a car.

Now she seemed pleased and more relaxed.

Jesse wanted, he realized, to show this woman so much more than his brother's ranch. He wanted to show her London and Paris and anyplace else she'd like to see.

Actually, he wanted to make up for every moment of fear or deprivation or loneliness she'd ever known.

If he could have erased every heartbreak from her past, he would have done it, then and there, no matter what the cost.

"You look so serious," she remarked. "What's on your mind?"

Jesse hadn't realized she was watching him. "Stuff," he said.

"*Stuff?*" she asked.

"You. I was thinking about what it's been like for you…" He glanced into the rearview mirror at Isabel, who was having a serious conversation with Norvel about what a nice dog he was. "All the things you told me last night."

"It's worrisome at times," she said carefully, "but I'll cope. I always have."

"But you're tired. You said so last night."

"Lots of people are tired," she replied. "It's part of the human condition."

"We still need to speak with Eli as soon as possible," he said.

"I know," she answered with a sigh, "but can we just forget about all that for now? The sun is shining and the countryside is so beautiful and it's lovely to get away for a little while."

They'd reached the top of Liam's driveway, which, unlike the roads they'd just traveled, was paved.

Liam's house appeared in the distance, low and rambling, with a portico.

"Wow," Tessa said on a long breath. "Is your brother a movie star or something?"

Jesse laughed. "No," he said. "He's an architect with a knack for managing money—and a trust fund."

He saw her throat move as she swallowed that information.

And he knew what she wanted to ask next, and that she wouldn't allow herself to do it.

"Yes," he said quietly. "I have a trust fund, too."

"So do I!" Isabel put in, from her car-seat perch in back. "I'm going to college *for sure*!"

The child's interjection broke the mild tension that

had settled between Jesse and Tessa in the last few moments.

"Have you decided on a major yet?" Jesse teased, grinning.

"I want to be a mommy, with a whole bunch of kids and dogs and ponies!"

Tessa laughed. "Three days ago, Isabel Stafford, you told me you wanted to be Annie Oakley. And last week, you were planning to become an astronaut."

"There are lots of choices," Isabel admitted. "But I can't be Annie Oakley because Teacher says somebody else already was."

"She knows about Annie Oakley? And space travel?" Jesse inquired, amused. "At *five years old*?"

"I'm almost six," Isabel pointed out, as though that explained everything.

"I told you before," Tessa said to Jesse. "We're suckers for old Westerns. And she loves learning about astronauts."

They passed the main house, then the barn, and came to a stop in front of the guesthouse, which Liam referred to as "the cottage."

"This is where I live," Jesse said, feeling a little self-conscious now, though he couldn't have explained that for anything. "In the guest quarters."

Tessa leaned forward, studying the place through the windshield. "This is *some* guesthouse," she pointed out.

"Liam likes to entertain," Jesse said. "The main house has seven bedrooms. The cottage is for the overflow, I guess."

"Evidently," Tessa murmured. "Why isn't he living on the ranch?"

"He'll get around to moving in," Jesse replied, getting out of the truck and going around to open the passenger door for Tessa.

Once she was standing in the frosty grass, pulling her coat closer around her as the wind picked up, he released Norvel and unbuckled Isabel from the booster seat.

Norvel, as was his custom, ran wildly around in circles, unable to contain his joy at being set free.

Laughing, Isabel chased after him, holding her arms out as though she might take wing and fly.

Like breakfast in Tessa's kitchen, this was a moment Jesse never wanted to forget.

Tessa surprised him by linking her arm loosely through his.

"Thank you, Jesse," she said very quietly.

He looked down at her, smiling quizzically. "For?"

She shrugged her slender shoulders, and her smile

faltered slightly. "Being kind—sleeping on my ratty old sofa so you could protect us. Taking us to Bitter Gulch ahead of the rush. And now a visit to your brother's ranch. Isabel and I haven't had much of a chance to make memories like this before."

He wanted to kiss her.

But he didn't move.

She was shy. She'd had to be vigilant, 24/7. She was like a bird, skittish. Ever ready to catch the wind and let it carry her away.

If he moved too fast, she'd be as good as gone, even if she stayed on in Painted Pony Creek for the rest of her life.

So he was careful.

Casual.

Hospitable.

"Come on," he said gruffly after several moments spent searching his mind for a reply besides *You're welcome*. "We'll start with the barn, so Isabel can have a look at Max, the pony, and maybe sit on his back for a few minutes."

She nodded, looking as though she'd wanted to say something more and had chosen not to for reasons of her own.

There were twelve stalls in Liam's fancy barn, all of

them empty at the moment, though once his brother settled in to stay, the place would be crowded.

Max, the Shetland, was in the nearby pasture, along with Wildfire, Jesse's treasured gelding.

Jesse went to the white rail fence, put his thumb and index finger to his mouth and whistled.

Isabel and Norvel had joined him and Tessa by then.

The little girl scrambled up onto the lowest fence rail, peering through the gap at the rapidly approaching horses.

A brown-and-white pinto, broad in the barrel because of all the treats he'd been given, Max came straight to Isabel and unleashed all his charms on her. Max was a pampered little beast—he'd belonged to Liam's kids since they were babies, spending most of his life on the family ranch outside Olive Grove—but he was good-natured and friendly.

The child was barely able to stand still. She reached out to pat the pony's muzzle, tentatively at first.

Max nickered and tossed his head. His mane was tangled, since he was overdue for some grooming, and that, coupled with his girth, made him look a little like a hooligan.

Jesse looked to Tessa, silently asking permission,

and after a few moments of solemn consideration, she nodded.

Jesse swept Isabel up into his arms.

"Want to ride him?"

Isabel nodded fervently.

Jesse opened the gate and carried her through, setting her on Max's wide, bare back.

Isabel clung to his wild mane with both hands, eyes bright with excitement.

Soon she was riding around and around in a wide circle, Jesse close by her side, ready to catch her if she fell.

❄ 7 ❄

For the next few days, Jesse sheltered Tessa and Isabel from all possible harm, and though the necessity of it chafed her considerable pride, Tessa cooperated. She knew it couldn't last.

Mostly, it was business as usual. She worked her shifts at Bailey's, and Isabel attended kindergarten and day care under the watchful supervision of her teacher and the childcare workers.

After work, Jesse slept at Tessa's some nights, tossing and turning on that awful couch. Other times, Tessa and Isabel stayed in the cottage on the ranch, in the spacious spare room just down the hall from Jesse's bedroom.

Tessa was getting too comfortable, too complacent,

and she knew it, but she couldn't help indulging in the semi-fantasy of having a real home and a partner.

On the ranch, the three of them passed whole evenings playing board games and watching old movies on the big flat-screen in Jesse's living room. After Isabel went to sleep, they talked. Jesse told Tessa what it was like to grow up on a working ranch. Tessa told *him* about her mother, the various foster homes she'd lived in. Of course, her life hadn't *all* been dreary and dysfunctional. Most of the foster parents were kind enough. And about the Staffords, the couple who had taken her in, loved her like their own and then died in an accident.

She'd had friends, even before she went to live with the Staffords, and she'd gotten good grades. In high school, she'd been a cheerleader and a member of the National Honor Society, landing several small but much-needed scholarships, and her foster parents had seen to it that she got therapy.

Jesse simply listened. He never asked for more than she was willing to tell, and he didn't make judgments.

Best of all, much to Tessa's relief, he didn't seem to feel sorry for her.

Instead, he admired her for her strength and courage.

Tessa wasn't sure she agreed with that assessment;

she'd been scared for much of her life, even when things were going well.

There was always that need to stay ahead of the curve, lest some disaster overtake her without warning. Which, of course, disasters usually did, and at the most unexpected times.

What she *hadn't* told Jesse was that she'd started getting counseling at the community clinic—preliminary diagnosis, low self-esteem, among other things—or that she was on birth control now.

The time they'd spent together since she'd asked Jesse to come over that first evening had been innocent—on the surface.

They were careful, because of Isabel, not to touch and definitely not to kiss.

Still, the atmosphere crackled between them, and when they occasionally bumped into each other, both of them flinched and said *Sorry*.

It was, Tessa was beginning to think, ridiculous.

Jesse was a man, and she was a woman, and though they hadn't said so, they wanted each other.

Damn, but Tessa yearned to be alone with Jesse, just the two of them, and find out how deep their attraction ran.

She had the day of the Thanksgiving dance off. That

morning, she washed her hair and slathered herself with body lotion. She shaved her legs and armpits. She rooted through her small collection of makeup, most of which was probably past its expiration date, and was happy to find a tube of red lipstick, some blusher and a small palette of shimmery eye shadow that would work well with her borrowed dress.

Ah, the dress.

It fit her perfectly, thanks to Miranda, and when she tried it on with a pair of red pumps she'd found packed among her few belongings, she felt like a different person.

No, she decided, standing there in her still-steamy bathroom, wrapped in a towel with her hair dripping wet, *not* like a different person, but like the person she truly was, down deep, under all the fears and doubts and misgivings.

The person she was meant to be.

She'd only been to two therapy sessions so far, but the volunteer counselor, a middle-aged social worker named Mary Collins, had reminded her that she was more than a mommy, more than a food service worker, more than a college dropout who'd passed much of her adult life on the open road, trying to outrun Marjory Laughlin.

She was a *woman*, first and foremost, a valuable human being with a lot to offer the world. Whether she married or stayed single, worked the rest of her days waiting tables or started the long road to a college degree in elementary education, she was important, deserving of respect.

She'd known, once she'd managed to shut down the critical voice in her head, that Ms. Collins was right.

As callous as he'd been, Brent wasn't her problem.

Marjory, though still a formidable foe, hadn't undermined Tessa's worth in any real way.

No, Tessa had done that herself.

I have choices.

The realization, so long suppressed, had left her thunderstruck.

She could deal with Marjory—and with anyone else who tried to come between her and her child.

She'd already taken steps to put an end to Marjory Laughlin's harassment, with Jesse's help, alerting both Sheriff Garrett and Melba to the possibility that the woman or some of her henchmen might try to abduct Isabel *or* do bodily harm to Tessa.

Now there was a restraining order in place, and Sheriff Garrett's deputies were keeping an eye out for any kind of trouble.

Still, it was only when she was with Jesse that Tessa felt sure that she and Isabel were completely safe. Though she knew, from Miranda, that the entire town felt protective toward the newest single mom in town and her funny, smart little girl.

And that gave Tessa a feeling of belonging that she'd never known before in any of the cities and towns she'd passed through, and she didn't want to leave the Creek, no matter what.

Just before noon, fat flakes of snow began to drift down from the heavy gray sky. Isabel was thrilled.

It had been decided that Carly would pick the little girl up after lunch and take her home to the Hollister ranch, where Carly's parents, Cord and Shallie, would help to look after Isabel. They had a new baby in the house, and they'd decided to skip the big dance this time around.

Isabel was getting her slumber party, finally, and she was tickled to death at the prospect.

Like Jesse's place, the Hollister ranch had horses; dogs, too. Carly had a big, girlie bedroom, by her account, and she and Isabel would sleep in canopy beds placed side by side.

Now, back in her customary jeans, sneakers and T-shirt, Tessa made tuna sandwiches and chicken noodle soup for lunch. Isabel zipped around the house, now chatting in the kitchen, now at the front window, now checking and rechecking the things she'd packed for the visit. All the while she chattered away about all she and Carly were going to do—play video games, eat homemade pizza and maybe even ride a horse, a really gentle one, chosen especially for Isabel.

Tessa summoned her to the table for lunch and sat down to join her.

"Do you think the snow will stick, Mommy?" Isabel asked, kicking the chair legs with her heels. "Jesse said we could go sledding and have a bonfire and *everything*, as soon as there's enough snow."

At his request, Isabel had stopped calling him "Mr. McKettrick."

"Stop kicking the chair," Tessa said calmly. "And I don't know if the snow will stick or melt away by the end of the day. Snow is tricky stuff."

"What if there's no snow when it's Christmas Eve?" Isabel pressed, somewhat anxious now. "What will Santa do then?"

"Santa is a resourceful fellow," Tessa assured her, hiding a smile, thinking of the dollhouse family she'd found at Vintage Treasures. Miranda had reclothed the lot of them, in style, and Tessa had been so pleased that she'd shown them to Jesse when Isabel was in bed.

He was building an elaborate dollhouse to accommodate them, as a gift for Isabel.

"Does 'russ-orse-full' mean he'll come no matter what?"

"Yes, that's what it means, buttercup. Eat your lunch." Then she repeated the word "resourceful," syllable by syllable, and gave a proper definition so Isabel could store the information away in that busy little brain of hers.

"*You're* resourceful, Mommy," Isabel said matter-of-factly. "You can make things work even when they don't want to."

Tessa thought of her car, still moldering in the garage. Sighed.

"Not always," she replied.

Isabel dug in her figurative heels. Shook her head earnestly. "Always," she insisted. "When I'm all grown up, I want to be the same kind of mommy you are."

Tessa's eyes stung, and she sniffled. Focused on her food.

"Eat your lunch," she said for the second time.

Carly arrived, bundled up and beaming, just as they finished their meal.

If she minded babysitting on an evening when most of her friends were probably heading for the Thanksgiving dance, she gave no sign of it.

"Time to bring out the jingle bells," Carly said to Isabel, who shamelessly adored the girl. "Next thing you know, Santa will be stopping by."

Tessa felt a stab of affection for Carly Hollister. Not to mention gratitude. There were huge snowflakes resting on her shoulders and sleeves and dappling her knit cap, and she seemed genuinely pleased to see Isabel, even though they spent most afternoons together at Bailey's.

After a lot of hustle and bustle, Isabel and Carly left the house, headed for Carly's small, snow-speckled compact car, parked at the curb.

Isabel's eager chatter faded, and Tessa closed the door against the cold wind, locked it.

For a moment, she worried—it was systemic with her—because, even though she knew the Hollister family fairly well, it was still difficult to let Isabel out of her sight. But then she reminded herself that she mustn't smother the little girl.

Scare her though it might, she had to give Isabel *some* leeway, time in other places with other people.

Marjory had taken so much from them, robbing Tessa of peace and Isabel of simple freedoms.

She straightened, squared her shoulders.

She was through letting Marjory intimidate her.

She'd found Painted Pony Creek, with all its friendly, caring people, and she and Isabel weren't leaving.

For the next few hours, she rehearsed the new Tessa.

The strong, confident Tessa.

She whisked up an egg-white face mask and sliced a cucumber. Then she lay on her bed, mask on her face and cukes cooling her eyes.

Tonight, she would look her best—even if it killed her.

With that thought in mind, she drifted off into sleep and dreamed that Bitter Gulch was a real place, that Jesse was the town marshal and she was a dance-hall girl, clad in sparkles, trying to win his heart.

She danced just for him in the saloon, prancing up and down the bar in a short, ruffly red dress. He held out his arms and she leaped into them, and there were cheers aplenty as he carried her up the back stairs.

Tessa woke with a heated jolt, feeling her cheeks burn beneath the dried mask. She ached for the real, flesh-and-blood Jesse, with his quiet, manly ways, his strong, lean body, his expressive eyes, his thick, brownish-blond hair.

She gasped and jumped up from the bed, breathing hard, as though she had just been chased by something fast.

"Breathe," she told herself. "It was just a dream."

Just a dream.

Her heart pounded and blood thundered in her ears.

One hand pressed to her sternum, she breathed. Breathed again.

It had happened because she was spending so much time with Jesse, at her place and at his. She'd let her imagination run away from her too many times, and the dream was proof that she needed to step back.

Calmer, but still a little dizzy, she lowered her head between her knees and consciously tried to rein in her heart, her lungs, her mind.

When she dared to stand up, two circles of cucumber, heretofore stuck to her T-shirt, dropped to the floor.

She picked them up and tossed them into the garbage, frustrated with herself.

She still felt a very focused ache, hot and fierce.

She washed the mask off her face.

She paced.

She took a cold shower.

She lectured herself.

And nothing changed. Her mind wanted to step

lightly around Jesse McKettrick, but her body lobbied to take him down—the sooner, the better.

When it was time to get ready for the dance, Tessa was still under the dream spell, though she probably appeared calm enough as she went about putting on her makeup, spritzing herself lightly with perfume.

After that, she donned the magical red dress. Pinned her hair up, leaving tendrils to dangle from the sides, as instructed by Miranda and Melba.

She barely recognized the woman gazing back at her from the full-length mirror on the inside of the bathroom door.

This wasn't shy, practical, semi-paranoid Tessa Stafford.

This was the dance-hall girl Tessa, the dance-on-the-bar Tessa, the carry-me-up-the-stairs-to-the-first-bedroom-you-see Tessa.

Jesse's knock sounded at the front door, and she started. Took a few breaths to steady her nerves.

Time to rock and roll.

Jesse was thinking about the forecast while he waited on Tessa's porch; it called for as much as twelve inches of snow in the next few hours.

He heard footsteps on the other side of the front door

and sucked in a deep breath. He felt like a teenager, taking the prettiest girl in school to the prom.

Maybe he should have picked up a corsage?

The door opened with a creak and there was Tessa, in all her sweet, sexy glory, dressed to kill.

He was stunned to silence by the sight of her in that curve-hugging red dress, with the neckline plunging just enough to hint at cleavage.

She took in his bespoke suit, the only one he'd brought from his condo in California in case of weddings and funerals, and her shining brown eyes widened.

"Come in," she said with a smile that warmed him through, like a shot of good whiskey on a freezing-cold night.

Jesse managed to recover enough equanimity to step over the threshold.

"Would you mind fastening this for me?" she asked, holding up a dainty gold necklace. The pendant was a tiny heart. "I can't seem to do it with my hands behind my head."

Jesse paused long enough to relish the image of Tessa standing with her hands behind her head.

"Um—sure," he said.

She handed him the necklace and turned her back.

He stood there, stricken, holding the jewelry. It took all his willpower not to kiss her nape, nibble at the side of her neck, forget all about the dance and coax her out of that eff-me red dress and let nature take its course.

Instead, after three or four tries, he managed to close the clasp.

The urge to pat her silk-draped backside was almost overwhelming, and the scent of her perfume made him a little dizzy.

She turned to face him, smiled again.

"Thanks," she said.

Her lips were plump and red.

Again, he wanted to kiss her.

Again, he restrained himself.

"Isabel is with Carly?" he asked, though he already knew the answer.

"Yes," Tessa replied, guileless. If she'd picked up on the undercurrent to his question, she didn't show it.

Jesse took her coat from its place by the door and helped her into it.

Then he looked down at her feet.

"Do you have snow boots?" he asked. "It's deep out there."

Tessa shook her head, looking vaguely embarrassed.

"Then I guess I'll have to carry you to the car," he said.

They stood on the porch while Jesse took Tessa's key and locked the door.

Tessa was peering through the thick, swirling snow at the car, parked by the curb. "You didn't bring the truck?" she asked. Once again, when she turned to look at him, her eyes were wide. Liam kept his Porsche at the ranch, and Jesse had borrowed it for the evening. Hoped it wouldn't turn into a pumpkin at midnight.

"We can swap out the car if you want. That would mean driving out to the ranch first, of course, and missing dinner and the opening dance."

Her smile was quick—and dazzlingly bright. "I've never ridden in a car like that," she said, barely concealing her excitement.

"Not even with Brent?" he asked, raising the collar of her coat around her face in a probably futile effort to keep her warm.

"Definitely not with Brent," she replied. "He drove a classic car—a convertible."

"Hmm," Jesse said. Then, without warning, he lifted Tessa into his arms and carried her down the steps, along the short, snowy walkway and around to the passenger side of the car.

She felt feather light in his arms, and she laughed with delight, tilting her head back to let the snowflakes catch on her cheeks and chin and forehead.

It was in those moments, in that brief, magical slice of eternity, that Jesse McKettrick knew, for a fact, that he'd fallen in love—not again, but for the first time ever.

Opening the car door with a sexy woman in his arms was awkward, but Jesse managed it, even though his head was running wild like a herd of mustangs on the first day of a long-awaited spring.

He set Tessa in the passenger seat, shut the door and slogged around to the driver's side.

"Before you get all impressed," he said once he was behind the wheel and the powerful engine was running, "this is Liam's car."

Tessa settled in, fastened her seat belt and then looked over at Jesse as they pulled away from the curb. "This is an amazing ride," she said mildly, "and you're looking better than fantastic in that suit, but the truth is, I like riding in your pickup truck, with you in jeans and a T-shirt and a denim jacket."

Pleased, Jesse digested that statement in silence as he drove through the flurry-filled streets of Painted Pony Creek.

When they arrived at the high school gym, practically every parking place was taken—there were trucks, cars, vans everywhere, along with a few motorcycles and even a tractor.

"Somebody was determined to come to the dance," Tessa observed.

Jesse laughed. "Must have been a cold ride into town," he added.

"And slow," she quipped.

He helped Tessa out of the car and into the building before parking Liam's Porsche at some distance from the gym and sprinting back.

Inside, he found her quickly, chatting with Alice and Mike Bailey, champagne in hand. The older couple had dressed in their Sunday best; Alice wore a corsage of red carnations and Mike sported a matching boutonniere.

Tables had been set up all around, and a light supper was to be served before the dancing started at eight o'clock. They found their table, and jovial crowds ebbed and flowed all around them; greetings were exchanged and there was plenty of laughter.

These were country people, and they enjoyed holidays and gatherings like this one to the fullest. Instead of jamming Halloween, Thanksgiving, Christmas and New Year's into one big, obnoxious tangle of commercialism, the residents of Painted Pony Creek and the neighboring Silver Hills took their time and celebrated each one in its turn.

That made sense to Jesse.

He wasn't one to rush things, either.

He glanced at Tessa, sitting shyly but happily at his side, and thought of that moment back at the house when he'd carried her to the car.

Yes, he loved her.

And, yes, it was too soon to get serious.

He felt exhilarated and sad, both at once.

When dinner was over and it was time for the dancing to begin, he offered Tessa his arm and she took it.

The gymnasium floor had been covered with thin tarps to protect the basketball court beneath, and the bleachers were folded against the walls to make room for the special decorations and the happy crowd.

Tessa drew in her breath when she first saw the spectacle—the space was encircled by winter-white trees gleaming with fairy lights, and fake snow lay in graceful heaps around their trunks. Dark netting of some kind hung from the ceilings, with hundreds of silver stars interwoven, casting a glimmer of their own over the heads of the dancers beneath.

A small orchestra imported all the way from Helena was on the stage, playing soft, wintry tunes. Jesse pulled Tessa into a slow waltz, and his heart leaped at the feel of her body pressed close to his.

"I was expecting big turkeys," Tessa confided, "like the one on top of the hardware store."

Jesse chuckled. "There wouldn't have been any room left for dancing," he replied.

"It's so—elegant," she whispered, as if spellbound. "Is there another dinner dance at Christmas?"

"Not as far as I know," he answered. "Last year, there was the tree lighting in the center of town, and the Methodist church had a living Nativity scene on their playground. That was something. Mary, Joseph, the baby—the whole crew, including kings and camels."

Tessa's eyes opened so wide that Jesse barely managed not to kiss her, then and there, in front of God and everybody. "Camels?" she marveled. "*Real* ones, or just horses in costumes?"

He grinned, enjoying the thought of horses dressed up as camels. "Real ones. There's a guy over by Silver Hills who raises them. Lets people ride them for a price, and rents them out for events. Movies, too."

"But it's so cold here," Tessa said, fretting. "Aren't camels strictly desert animals?"

"They're pretty rugged, actually," Jesse replied, still

amused—and touched—by the wonder in her brown, brown eyes. "These particular animals are well taken care of, anyway."

They moved together to the music for a while, without speaking, touching and pulling away, touching and pulling away.

It was driving Jesse crazy.

"How would you feel about leaving early?" he ventured when he'd endured the unintentional bait and switch for as long as he could without losing his mind.

Her smile nearly knocked him back on his heels. "I'd like that," she said. "But where will we go?"

Jesse risked it. Risked everything.

"My place?" he asked.

She stroked his right cheek, just once and very lightly. "Okay," she said.

They were out of the building and seated in the Porsche within minutes.

The snow was reaching blizzard proportions now, coming down in thick curtains that practically blocked out the gym, the parking lot and the other cars.

Jesse cursed himself silently for not bringing the truck. The Porsche was a masterpiece of automotive engineering, but it was built for speed, not country roads in a snowstorm.

Tessa didn't seem worried about the weather at all. She'd taken her phone from her handbag and was checking texts.

"Isabel's having a great time," she reported, smiling as Jesse navigated carefully out of the parking lot and onto the road. The screen lit up her face. "Carly says they might be snowed in by morning, though, and wants to know if I'd mind leaving Isabel at the Hollisters' ranch until it lets up."

The snowplows would be out soon, and Cord Hollister, one of the most prosperous ranchers in the area, surely had road-clearing equipment of his own, but if the storm meant he could be alone with Tessa for a night or two, well, so be it.

He gave an inward *yahoo*, but kept his expression serious.

After all, they had five miles of blinding snow flurries ahead of them.

"Jesse?" Tessa had put away her phone, and her voice was quiet. Uncertain.

"What?" he asked companionably.

"This isn't the kind of thing I do."

"What isn't the kind of thing you do?"

"I don't go home with men after a date."

He glanced her way, saw that she was nervous. "Nothing has to happen if you don't want it to, Tess," he told her. "We can do what we've *been* doing—watching movies, playing games, whatever works for you."

"It just seems kind of—well—*soon*, that's all."

To Jesse, nothing about that night was happening too soon. He felt as though he'd been waiting for this woman for a hundred lifetimes.

"Okay," he said, and his voice came out hoarse. He cleared his throat.

"I had a dream about us this afternoon when I lay down for a nap," she confided. "We were in Bitter Gulch, in the saloon, and it was all real—it was an actual town. You were the town marshal and I was a dance-hall girl and—"

Jesse shifted uncomfortably in the driver's seat, glad it was mostly dark except for the series of lights on the dashboard.

"Interesting," he said, barely suppressing a groan.

"Are you feeling all right?" Tessa asked innocently.

He couldn't tell her he'd gone hard as a crowbar, just at the mention of her sexy dream/fantasy.

"Oh, I'm great—just great."

She reached over, rested a concerned hand lightly on his thigh.

A jolt went through him, and his reaction was harder still to hide.

"It was quite a dream," she went on, sounding both determined and shy. "I was dancing on top of the bar and people were calling out and cheering, and I jumped and landed in your arms. And you—you carried me up the stairs—"

"Is that right?" he all but croaked.

He considered taking Tessa straight to Bitter Gulch. To the hotel, though the picture of her dancing on the saloon bar in a skimpy dress was seared into his brain.

They could break in the honeymoon suite.

But, no. The horses would need to be fed in the morning, and poor old Norvel was out there in the guesthouse, all by his lonesome.

Jesse had left him enough food and water, but the poor critter suffered from separation anxiety sometimes, and he'd need to go outside at some point.

Damn.

It took the better part of an hour to cover the seven-plus miles between the Creek and the ranch, and during that time, neither of them mentioned Tessa's afternoon dream.

Tessa, possibly thinking she'd said too much, was quiet.

Jesse asked if she wanted to stop by her house to pack an overnight bag.

She shook her head. She'd left a change of clothes in his guest room during one of her and Isabel's overnight visits, along with pajamas and toothbrushes.

He was, he concluded, thoroughly rattled. Still felt a little like that kid who'd just taken his girl to the big dance.

And like that kid, he didn't have a clue what to do next.

Pretend there wasn't a continuous sexual charge between them?

Or carry Tess straight through the house to his bedroom and peel that red dress off her in one swift move?

When they reached the ranch and he dropped Tessa off at the cottage while he put Liam's car away in the main house's garage, the figurative jury was still out.

❄ 8 ❄

"What have you gotten yourself into, Tessa Stafford?"

She was standing in the guest bathroom in the cottage, staring at her reflection in the long mirror over the sinks.

The color was high in her cheeks, and her eyes were overly bright with—what? Anticipation? Nerves?

She was barefoot now, but still in her borrowed red dress. Her carefully loose bun was looser still, leaning slightly to one side of her head, and it was damp from the trek between the car and the gym and then the house.

Not that she'd done much trekking. Jesse had mostly carried her.

The memory made the base of her throat throb.

She had *loved* being swept up into those strong arms, Rhett Butler–Scarlett O'Hara style.

What kind of modern, independent woman enjoyed being carried?

She did, though she doubted it would have been the same with any man besides Jesse McKettrick. Certainly none of her previous dates had done such a thing.

Only Jesse.

While she was still trying to work through all that, Jesse materialized in the bathroom doorway. He looked as though he'd been bewitched by some nymph of winter; his hair was mussed and he'd shed his coat and swapped out his suit for jeans and a flannel shirt.

Something ground almost painfully within Tessa, a terrible, beautiful desire, long frozen but now breaking free.

She didn't turn to face Jesse, though she held his gaze as they both stared into the mirror.

"Do you need anything?" he asked gruffly after a long silence.

Do I need anything?

Only to be held, to be touched, to be kissed and then kissed again.

Over the last four years on the road, she hadn't dared allow herself to think beyond keeping her child safe, keeping her fed and sheltered, always aware of the need to stay ahead of Marjory, running, running.

Continually broke or very close to it. Terrified, with every mile that rolled under her bald tires, that her car would break down.

All that while somehow keeping up a cheerful facade for her daughter's sake.

Down deep, she'd been starved for adult companionship, grown-up conversations about books and world affairs and a myriad of other interests.

She loved Isabel as much as any woman could love a child, but during her many talks with Jesse over the past week, serious and otherwise, she'd come to realize she needed more.

Just keeping her head above water wasn't enough.

Did that make her a bad mother?

A bad *person*?

Now, standing there in that sexy dress, alone and possibly snowbound with Jesse, reality caught up and cornered her.

Her mind needed Jesse's, needed his humor, his intelligence, his solid personal values, his quiet confidence and masculine ways.

Moreover, her body needed his.

Tonight, she wasn't a mom.

She wasn't a food service worker.

She wasn't in survival mode.

She was a flesh-and-blood woman.

"Do you need anything, Tess?" Jesse asked again, which was a good thing, because she'd forgotten the question.

"The zipper," she replied, never breaking eye contact with Jesse. A smile flickered across her mouth. "I managed to pull it up on my own, using an open safety pin and a string, but—"

"Very resourceful," Jesse answered, taking a step nearer.

"I'm used to making do," Tessa said.

He studied her face in the mirror for several moments before resting his hands lightly at her nape.

"You're sure about this?" he asked, trailing a kiss along the side of her neck without waiting for an answer.

He *knew* she was more than ready.

If she'd shown so much as a hint of reluctance, Jesse would have kept his distance.

She trembled, closed her eyes briefly. "I'm sure," she confirmed.

He slid the zipper down, very slowly, and she felt the tips of his fingers brush down her spine as he laid it bare. The way the dress was styled, she hadn't needed to wear a bra.

Her eyes fell closed again as a groan escaped her.

"Open your eyes," Jesse said gently. "I want you to see how beautiful you are."

"Jesse, I—"

"Shh," he said, watching her, and himself, as he slid the bodice of the dress downward, millimeter by millimeter, until her breasts were revealed.

Her nipples immediately hardened and she groaned again.

"Don't close your eyes," he whispered, kissing her shoulders now, first one side and then the other.

Tessa watched herself, watched Jesse. Swallowed hard.

She gasped his name when his strong, work-toughened hands cupped her breasts ever so gently, the pads of his thumbs lightly brushing her nipples.

She was flushed pink, from her waist to her hairline, and her breaths were quick and shallow.

If this was foreplay, she reflected feverishly, she didn't know how she would bear the final climax. She already felt as though she would explode, like a dying star flinging shards of fire in all directions.

When they finally collided, a whole new universe might be created.

"Mmm," Jesse murmured, as he continued to caress her breasts to drive her crazy. "You're even more beautiful when you're aroused," he said, his voice low and maybe a touch more urgent.

If Tessa had one clear thought in those moments, it was that Jesse McKettrick liked to take his time.

She whimpered. How could she possibly wait?

Jesse seemed to read her mind; he chuckled, a throaty sound, and eased the dress over her hips and thighs, letting it drift to the floor.

She shivered, electrified.

She started to turn around, wanting Jesse's kiss as well as his touch, but he stopped her. Pushed her panties down, parting her, playing with her.

She dropped her head back against his shoulder. "Oh, Jesse—kiss me—*please*."

"Soon," he replied, but he kept on fondling her, driving her higher and higher, nearer and nearer the edge of the precipice.

Tessa was sure she was about to disintegrate.

The motion of Jesse's fingers was slow, and she was moist with need for him.

And then it happened.

The entire cosmos splintered into blazing fragments.

Tessa cried out, pressing back into Jesse's midsection, feeling his erection at the small of her back.

Jesse whispered sweet encouragements to her as her body buckled, again and again, as though pitched from one side of creation to the other.

When the delicious seizing finally stopped, her knees wobbled, and Jesse caught her by the waist.

Held her up.

Turned her around.

And then he kissed her at such length, and with such thoroughness, that she knew she wouldn't be able to stand on her own.

She was faint with satisfaction, but new desires, new needs were awakening within her, too.

Jesse set her on the bathroom counter, checking that she was secure before recovering the discarded dress and hanging it over a hook on the back of the bathroom door. He left Tessa's panties where they were.

Facing her, he ran his strong carpenter's hands along her naked thighs. "You," he said, his voice almost ragged, "are beyond beautiful."

He kissed her again, lightly this time. Kissed her mouth and her forehead and both her eyes, and all the while, he was stroking her thighs.

They began to quiver.

She wrapped her arms around his neck, pulled him into a deeper kiss.

Now it was Jesse who moaned.

She opened his shirt, rested her palms against his muscular chest to feel his heartbeat, the form and substance of him.

When she sensed that he couldn't endure the waiting much longer, she smiled, feeling every bit the temptress, and pressed against him.

Jesse lifted her then, and, once again, he carried her.

This time, to his bed.

There, they made love in earnest.

They rested, dozed and made love again.

Jesse fell asleep first, and Tessa lay beside him, snug under the covers, with his warm, solid body spooning hers.

She watched through the bedroom window as more snow drifted down, the flakes as thick and white as dove feathers, rimmed in the faintest glow of moonlight.

Jesse was deep in slumber, and Tessa slipped out of his arms, careful not to wake him. Clearly, he'd exhausted himself loving her, and she didn't want to disturb his rest.

He looked strong and at the same time vulnerable as he slept.

Maybe, she mused, people were at their purest when they surrendered to sleep.

It was the waking mind, wasn't it, that stirred up drama?

Not that Jesse was the dramatic type. He was well-mannered and straightforward, and Tessa loved that about him.

She paused, tensed slightly. *Loved?*

Jesse was *GQ* good-looking, and he knew his way around a woman's body, that was for sure.

But *love*?

Had she been silly enough to let herself fall in love?

She'd wanted Jesse, that was for sure, and she'd reveled in his lovemaking, reveled in pleasing him, but genuine, grown-up *love*?

The kind that lasted?

Surely not.

You don't know the first thing about love, Tessa Stafford, lectured the tireless voice in her head. *Not the man-woman kind, anyway. You never even laid eyes on your bio-dad, who could have been anybody, including a one-night stand or the husband of one of Mom's friends. All you have to go by is the time you spent with Brent, and that was* never *love; it was wishful thinking. Delusion.*

Admit it. You wanted sex.

You got it.

Oh, boy, did you get it.

But what happens now?

An old cliché came to mind; ironically, she'd heard it from her blatantly promiscuous mother. *Why buy the cow when you can get the milk for free?*

She sat up, trying her best not to disturb Jesse, and got out of bed.

She crept out of his room, went down the hallway to the one she and Isabel had shared when they'd taken shelter here before.

She showered in the adjoining bathroom, brushed her teeth and donned the clothes she'd left behind on a previous visit. She combed her mist-dampened hair and headed for the kitchen.

Norvel, curled up on a rug to one side of the back door, eyed her companionably when she flipped on the lights.

"Hey, buddy," Tessa whispered. "Don't bark, okay?"

Norvel gave a great snort. Turned his head to one side, watching as she searched the cupboards for tea bags, found none and settled for a tall glass of water.

Standing at the sink, she looked out at the continuing snowfall.

If anything, it had picked up speed.

For her own sake, Tessa wouldn't mind being snowbound, since she would be with Jesse, but Isabel, much as she loved Carly, wasn't used to being separated from her mom.

Tessa retrieved her handbag, which she'd left in the small entryway, along with her shoes, and extracted her phone and its charger.

The battery was dead, so she plugged it in.

After a minute or so, the screen lit up.

There was a text from Melba.

Tessa's wary heart shinnied up into her throat and pounded there. Drummed in her ears.

I don't want to worry you, but I need to double-check that Isabel is with Carly Hollister, like you planned. Marjory Laughlin is in town, staying at the Rose Bower B & B. The owner called to tell me she was asking about you and Isabel.

Tessa froze. Quickly texted a reply, hoping Melba was still awake, though it was late. After midnight.

Isabel is with Carly, at the Hollister ranch, but this is not a good thing.

Luckily, Melba *was* awake. Off duty, but clearly on red alert. I tried to get in touch with Jesse when I couldn't reach you, but he didn't pick up.

Tessa's thoughts skittered back over the evening.

Like her, Jesse had probably forgotten all about his phone, given how busy they'd been.

Tessa felt a rush of chagrin, and silently castigated herself for thinking she could live like a normal woman, even for a night.

She punched in Melba's number, didn't bother with a "hello." "What should I do?" she cried.

Jesse appeared in the doorway leading to the living room, wearing sweatpants and nothing else.

"Nothing much you *can* do," Melba responded in her businesslike way. "The snow's too deep for anybody to go anywhere, tonight at least, and I know for a fact that the Laughlin woman doesn't know where to look for either you *or* Isabel." There was a pause. "You are with Jesse, aren't you?"

"Yes, I'm with Jesse," Tessa said, meeting his gaze.

He was frowning, but he didn't interrupt the conversation.

"Well, stay put," Melba ordered. "Eli and I will handle the Evil Mama Bear."

"But what about Isabel?"

"Isabel is with the Hollisters. She's *safe*, Tessa. Now that I know what's what, I'll call Cord and Shallie, give them a heads-up about what's going on. You go back to sleep. We'll talk in the morning. Figure out our next move."

"Sleep? Are you serious?" Tessa asked breathlessly.

"Yes," Melba replied. "I'm serious. The county's snowplows are out in force, but no sooner do they get a stretch of highway cleared than it fills up again. Country roads aren't a high priority at the moment, Tessa."

Tessa closed her eyes. Breathed.

Jesse stood behind her now, massaging her tight shoulders.

"I've got to get to Isabel," Tessa said fretfully. "I know the Hollisters are good people, and they'll protect her, but *Marjory*—"

"Ms. Laughlin is snowed in, like everyone else," Melba said, sounding calm. Reasonable. "As soon as there's a break in the weather, I'll head over to the B & B and make sure she knows there's a restraining order against her. If she comes within five hundred feet of you *or* Isabel, she'll be a guest at the county jail."

"She's *rich*, Melba! She'll simply bail herself out. You don't know this woman. She doesn't understand the word *no*, she's not entirely sane and *she wants Isabel*!"

"Let me talk to Jesse, if he's available," Melba said evenly.

The request stung; *she*, Tessa, was Isabel's mother. And here Melba was, passing the conversation off to a man.

Gently, Jesse took the phone. "Hey, Chief," he said. "I gather we've got trouble, right here in River City." He paused, listened. "All right. I'll make sure Tess doesn't go anywhere—not without me, anyhow." Another pause. "Okay. Thanks. Bye."

He ended the call, pulled a chair close to Tessa's, sat down and wrapped an arm around her shoulders.

She was hunched over, her hands covering her face.

"How well do you know Cord Hollister, Tess?" he asked presently, his voice husky.

Tessa lowered her hands.

"Not well," she replied, shaking her head. "Carly introduced me to her parents, and I've waited on him and his friends at Bailey's pretty often, but I can't say I know him at all—and now he's all that stands between Marjory and my little girl!"

He chuckled at the stubborn set of her mouth and smoothed her lips with the pad of his thumb, a visceral reminder that he'd done the same to her nipples a few hours earlier.

"Cord's a good man," Jesse went on. "He's been a rancher all his life, and he wrangles messed-up horses—dangerous horses—most days. Suffice it to say, he's more than a match for Marjory Laughlin."

"She might have brought goons," Tessa half whispered.

"If she has, they'll get a lesson on how unwise it is to tangle with a cowboy, born and bred, with a family and friends to protect."

Tessa's eyes filled, and a tear trickled down her right cheek.

"I can't stand this," she muttered.

"You can, and you will," Jesse replied, "because Isabel needs you to be strong, especially now. How do you think she'll feel if you call her in the morning, and she picks up on how scared you are? She takes her cues from *you*, Tessa. Make sure they're good ones."

She deflated a little, let her head fall forward, pressing her forehead into Jesse's shoulder. He massaged her nape. Some of her tension began to fade away.

"I need her here, Jesse," she confessed, her voice muffled by his warm flesh. "I need Isabel to be here."

"I know," he said very gently. "I know."

She began to cry, and he didn't shove a Kleenex at

her or try to make her cheer up. He just held her close as she let it out.

After a while, when her sniffles had subsided, Jesse lifted her chin with one index finger and looked into her eyes.

The moment sizzled, though the heat between them wasn't sexual this time. It was something more, something Tessa couldn't quite identify.

"Let's get some sleep," he said quietly. "First thing in the morning, you can call the Hollister place and talk to the princess. I'll bet she's having a fine time over there with Carly and the younger kids. If I recall correctly, they have two little boys, and the second one is brand-new. Isabel likes babies, doesn't she?"

Tessa sniffled once more, nodded, managed a watery smile. "She asked for a little brother or sister for her birthday and Christmas."

Something sparked in Jesse's eyes. "Really? What did you tell her?"

"That a mommy can't make a baby all by herself. She needs a daddy to do that," Tessa recalled, buoyed by the memory. It was so very *Isabel*.

There was a solemnity to Jesse's expression, a kind of wariness, though the question he asked was blunt.

"Would you have more kids—if you met the right man?"

Was he talking about…?

Did he mean, would she have babies with *him*?

"I'd love to have more children," she said after biting her lower lip and thinking for a while. "But I'm pretty picky about the daddy part."

She couldn't read his expression, but she saw the tiniest muscle quirk at one side of his fine mouth and then relax again.

"That's good," he said.

And then he stood up without another word and offered Tessa his hand.

She took it, and he led her back to bed.

Four full days went by before the roads were passable again, and even then they were dangerously slick.

It was Thanksgiving morning, and the sun was summer-bright, gleaming on the snow-draped pastures and fields.

Jesse had just finished feeding the horses, letting the truck warm up while he worked, when Cord Hollister arrived at the wheel of a vehicle much like Jesse's.

Isabel rode in the back seat, strapped into a booster

chair, and she waved merrily as Tessa ran—not walked—
ran to meet them.

Barely waiting for Cord to apply the brakes, Tessa
was tugging at the handle on the rear passenger door.

She heard the snap of the locks releasing, yanked the
door open and grabbed for Isabel, fumbling with the
straps and buckles and getting nowhere.

With a chuckle, Cord stepped up, freed the little girl
and handed her over to Tessa, who clung to the child
fit to crush her.

"Don't hug me so hard, Mommy," Isabel instructed
blithely. "I'm going to pop!"

Tessa laughed, planted a noisy kiss on her daughter's
pink cheek. "I missed you *very much*!" She turned to
look at Cord, a handsome, dark-haired man with the
bluest eyes she'd ever seen. "Thank you," she said.

Cord, who was dressed much like Jesse in boots,
jeans, a flannel shirt and a wool-lined denim jacket,
tugged at the brim of an imaginary hat. "You're entirely welcome," he said, turning to greet Jesse, who'd
shoveled a path between the barn and the guest cottage.

He reached Tessa's side and put his hand out to Cord,
and the two men shook.

"Obliged," Jesse said.

"No problem," Cord replied.

Men of few words, both of them.

"Carly has two little brothers," Isabel told her mother excitedly, "and one of them is a little, tiny *baby*. He won't even be one years old for *eleven whole months*!"

The adults laughed, and Isabel began to wiggle, which meant she wanted to be put down so she could stand on her own two feet.

Tessa invited Cord in for coffee, but he said he had to get back home, told Isabel goodbye and left.

Isabel scampered to greet Norvel, who was waiting in the open doorway, probably wondering at the foolishness of the humans for standing around in knee-deep snow when there was a warm house a few steps away.

Dog and child rubbed noses in the entryway as Tessa and Jesse stepped inside.

"What happens now?" Jesse asked in a voice too low for Isabel to catch.

Over the last few days, Tessa had talked of little besides getting Isabel back and subsequently confronting Marjory Laughlin, who was, according to Melba, still at the B & B, keeping a low profile, so he probably expected her to ask that he drive her to town.

Instead, she said, "We start cooking. It's Thanksgiving Day, Jesse."

He glanced sideways at Isabel, who was still preoccupied with the Norvel reunion, and gave Tessa a kiss, the nibbling kind that sent flashes of desire through her and made her ache, way down deep.

"Stop it," she said, though she was smiling and she felt a warm, spilling sensation low in her torso. "We need to get dinner started."

They wouldn't have a turkey, but that didn't matter to Tessa. She'd found three plump game hens in the freezer two days before, and they'd been thawing in the refrigerator ever since.

Having stated her plans—*their* plans—for the morning, she busied herself getting Isabel out of her coat, mittens and snow boots. Jesse had brought in her miniature pink suitcase. Later, Tessa would find that all the clothes inside had been freshly laundered, thanks to Carly.

"Are you hungry?" Jesse asked the little girl.

Isabel shook her head happily, making her blond pigtails sway. "We had breakfast at Carly's house," she said. "But my toes are *really* cold."

"Sounds like you need a warm bath," Tessa replied. "Come on. Let's get you ready for a nice Thanksgiving."

Isabel looked up at her with wide, eager eyes. "Are we going to stay *here*, Mommy, with Jesse and Norvel?"

"For now," Tessa said.

When she returned to the kitchen half an hour later, Jesse was standing at the kitchen sink, peeling potatoes.

He looked downright domestic—and sexy as all get-out.

He acknowledged Tessa and Isabel with a wink and a grin, though his phone was wedged between his right shoulder and his ear.

"Yes," he said to whoever was on the other end of the call. "I'll miss all of you, too."

Tessa felt a pang. He was talking to someone in his family. His mom? His dad? Maybe both of them?

For a fraction of a second, she was envious.

She and Isabel had always been on their own on holidays—and all the rest of the time.

"Sure," Jesse went on, "maybe next year. No—" he glanced Tessa's way briefly "—I don't think I'll make it home for Christmas, Mom. Liam and the kids will be there, right?…And Rhett and his girlfriend—what's her name again?…Molly…Right…Okay, let me talk to Dad." Pause. "No, Mom, I'm *not* all alone." His gaze caught Tessa's again, and she felt caressed by it. "It's going to be a great Thanksgiving—even without your deep-fried turkey."

Tessa realized she was essentially eavesdropping and

took Isabel's hand again, intending to get them both out of earshot.

Instead, Isabel broke free and took off for the living room with Norvel, and she was soon squealing with laughter.

"Yes, Mom," Jesse went on. "You heard right. I have company—give me a second." He beckoned to Tessa, set the phone down, wiped his hands, and she went to his side.

He put an arm around her middle, teased her a little by running the tip of his index finger beneath the waistband of her jeans.

"No, I'm not going to tell you who," he said. "We'll discuss my social life another time, if it's all the same to you."

Tessa swatted at his hand.

He tugged at the snap, pretending he was about to unbutton her pants.

She laughed and stepped back, out of reach, though if Isabel hadn't been there with them and playing in the living room, she would have interrupted the call between Jesse and his mom and led him straight to the bedroom.

He wasn't the only one who knew how to tease.

The call took another twenty minutes, during which

Tessa busied herself chopping onions and celery for stuffing. When that was done, she obsessed over the game hens, poking them, wondering if they were ready to wash, season and put into the oven.

Jesse ended the conversation with his family and set the phone on the counter. "You'll like my mother," he said.

"Norman Bates said the same thing, in *Psycho*," Tessa quipped.

Jesse laughed.

Tessa thought of Brent then, and Marjory, still hanging around Painted Pony Creek, despite the restraining order. As long as she kept the specified distance between herself and Tessa and Isabel, nothing much could be done.

Brent *hadn't* said she'd like his stepmother when he and Tessa got together; he hadn't even mentioned having one.

She went to the living room to check on Isabel and found her sitting on the floor, quietly playing a game of tug-of-war with Norvel. One of Jesse's socks played the role of the rope.

"Can I watch TV, Mommy?" Isabel asked. "There's a parade on, and it's over in New York City, but we can still see it here."

Figuring Jesse wouldn't mind, Tessa switched on the flat-screen TV above the fireplace and found the big parade.

A gigantic Mickey Mouse was passing along a crowded street, bouncing and bobbing like the turkey on top of the hardware store.

Tessa smiled and went back to the kitchen.

Jesse was leaning against the counter, a cup of coffee in hand. His eyes danced as he watched her.

"You're back," he joked. "I thought for sure you were going to stick me with all the cooking."

Tessa glanced at the large pot of sliced potatoes waiting to be boiled. "Seems to me you could handle the job with no trouble at all, cowboy," she replied.

He set the mug down, crossed to her and pulled her close.

Kissed her.

"Just call me Marshal McKettrick," he said. "Jump off the bar, in the saloon or anywhere else, and I'll catch you. No doubt about it."

❄ 9 ❄

Thanksgiving dinner was delicious even if it was a little nontraditional, and Tessa, Jesse and Isabel enjoyed it, and each other, seated in a semicircle at the round kitchen table.

Norvel, for his part, refrained from begging, though he did cruise past every few minutes, no doubt hoping for falling morsels of game hen or mashed potatoes or green bean casserole.

None came; Jesse had a rule against giving his dog people food, and he enforced it.

After dinner, Tessa and Jesse cleaned up together, while Isabel and Norvel wandered into the living room and promptly fell asleep in a heap on the floor.

Between spending time with the Hollisters and the

impromptu Thanksgiving at Jesse's, Isabel was tuckered out.

By six o'clock, it was completely dark, and Isabel couldn't keep her eyes open long enough to watch a holiday movie—*Christmas Vacation*—so Tessa took her back to the guest room, helped her get ready for bed and tucked her in.

Norvel accompanied them, curling up beside the bed.

Tessa couldn't help wondering if he'd somehow sensed the possibility that his little friend might be in danger and wanted to protect her.

Her heart cracked a little as she kissed Isabel's forehead and then leaned down to ruffle Norvel's floppy ears.

"Thanks, dude," she whispered.

Returning to the living room, Tessa plunked down on the couch beside Jesse. He draped an arm around her shoulders and muted the TV.

"Can you take us to town tomorrow morning?" Tessa asked, resting her head against his shoulder. "It's Black Friday, so Bailey's will be extra busy, and I've taken a lot of time off lately."

"What about Marjory?"

"I want to confront her," Tessa said. "But on my own

terms. It will all depend on the hours I'm scheduled to work tomorrow. *If* I'm scheduled to work. I could be fired for being a no-show for the last few days."

Jesse looked down into her upturned face, frowning a little. "Tessa, the whole county was snowed in. Bailey's probably wasn't even open for business. And I don't think Mike and Alice would let you go for something like that, anyway."

He could be forgiven for his easy assurance that things would go well; he hadn't been in her shoes, hadn't had to run from anything or anyone—or had he?

She sat up straighter and held his gaze. "Is there even the most remote possibility that *you* are on the run, too, Jesse? You live on your brother's ranch, drive his car when you don't want to use your truck. Nothing wrong with any of that, obviously, but I'm wondering what you're planning to do when Bitter Gulch is finished and open for business. You've never mentioned any plans beyond that, not in all the times we've talked."

He sighed, and though his expression was reluctant, he didn't look away. "I wouldn't say I'm running, exactly," he admitted. "I told you I'm divorced. What I didn't say was that I wanted kids and, out of the blue, Cynthia didn't. We'd dated since we were in high school, and we'd always planned on having a family. We hadn't been married too long and, to be fair, we were both fresh out of law school and working hard to get our careers off the ground, but one day, without any warning at all, Cynthia announces that she's changed her mind. No kids, not ever. She wanted to get on the fast track and become a partner in a few years.

"I was blindsided, but I figured it would blow over. She was under a lot of pressure to prove herself on the job and so was I.

"As things turned out, the chasm between us was too wide to cross. We made a mutual decision to divorce and go our own ways. That hurt, but I was bearing up okay, I guess. Working too hard to indulge in a lot of introspection.

"The divorce was barely final when, all of a sudden, Cynthia marries my best friend, Todd. I don't know if they cheated beforehand—maybe she just decided that being single wasn't what she wanted after all." Jesse paused, shoved a hand through his hair. "That really threw me, and Todd and I had a falling-out. It all seemed so sudden, she and Todd getting together, tying the knot and—"

"And then your godson came along?" Tessa said, taking his hand, passing her thumb back and forth against the range of his knuckles.

Jesse squeezed his eyes shut. "Yeah," he said. "I lost it, Tessa. I fell apart. She asked me to be the boy's godfather and I agreed. I tried to be a good godparent, but it hurt too much, and, naturally, Todd wasn't too crazy about the idea, either. He and I aren't on the best of terms, as you can probably imagine."

"So you came here, to Painted Pony Creek?" Tessa asked softly, watching his emotions play out on his face.

"That was Liam's idea," he replied after a long silence, during which he shifted his gaze from Tessa to the dying blaze in the big stone fireplace across the room. "I guess he figured I was on a greased track to hell or something, and being your typical older brother, he stepped in. Bought the land here, designed the house and barn and this place, and then, when that was done, he got the idea for Bitter Gulch. He likes the Creek, wants to finish raising his kids here—says all that sky is medicinal."

Tessa smiled. "Liam sounds like a good person."

"He is," Jesse said.

"What made him choose Painted Pony Creek?" Tessa ventured, then added with a twinkle, "Besides the big sky."

"He came here a few years ago, to learn about training horses. He worked with Cord Hollister, in fact. Always intended to come back and settle down, the whole bit. Only his wife, Waverly, got sick—*really* sick—and taking care of her and the kids and keeping his architecture firm afloat took up all his time."

"That's so sad," Tessa said, resting her palm lightly against Jesse's cheek.

Jesse gave a slight nod. His face was still grim.

"Eventually," he said after a brief silence, "Waverly left him. Took the kids and went to stay with her folks up in Seattle. I guess she thought she was too much of a burden or something, and Liam was wrecked, being separated from his dying wife and both their children, but he didn't fight the situation. Neither of them needed the stress, obviously."

"Waverly died?" Tessa asked.

"Yes, last year," Jesse answered. "The kids wanted to stay with their grandparents, although Liam sees them as often as he can. Now the in-laws are getting older, and the kids are getting harder to manage, so my brother decided to start all over again, right here."

Tessa could see that the plan didn't leave any room for Jesse, and once Bitter Gulch was up and running, he'd probably choose to move on, take on some other challenge, in some other place.

"What about your law practice?" she inquired carefully. It was all well and good that Jesse had chosen to confide in her, for whatever reason, but in actual fact, his plans were none of her business.

He sighed. "I think I took up the law because that was what Cynthia and I had agreed to do, way back in the day. I like it well enough, but, frankly, I don't need the money, and once I came here, I finally accepted the fact that I like building things more than taking depositions and going over contracts and filing lawsuits. I decided I'd get my license, just in case, and do pro bono work, when I thought it was right."

Jesse drew her closer to his side, kissed the top of her head.

"I'm sorry, Jesse," she told him, snuggling in. "That you were hurt, I mean. That your life didn't turn out the way you expected it would."

He gave a raspy chuckle, thereby lightening the mood. "Did yours?" he asked.

"Not exactly," she confessed. "I was going to become a teacher. Change the course of American education. Marry Clark Kent and have five or six super-children."

Jesse laughed at that, squeezed her against his side. "You could still be a teacher," he said.

"I guess I could," she replied seriously. "But, like you, I'm not sure I want to follow my original career plan, even if I could find the time and money. Which isn't likely. My real job, as I see it, is to hold space for Isabel—help her to grow up to be happy and smart and very, very secure in her own competence.

"Anyway, waiting tables isn't so bad. It's honest work, and I like it. And I love the people I meet—Mike and Alice and Miranda and Carly—and *most* of the customers."

Jesse turned to face her, taking her shoulders into his hands, but lightly, catching and holding her gaze.

"Isabel is one special little kid," he said, "but devoting your entire life to 'holding space' for her is going to leave you a little lonely, don't you think? What happens once she's a grown woman, off living her own life?"

Tessa swallowed. He wasn't criticizing her; she knew that.

So why did she feel just the tiniest bit guilty?

"Not everyone is meant to be a mover and a shaker, Jesse," she pointed out when she found the words. "The world needs worker bees, like me. What kind of planet would this be if *everybody* was some kind of wild success?"

He placed an index finger to her lips. "You're *already* a wild success," he said. "Especially as a mother." A short, thoughtful pause followed, though he continued to trace her mouth, as if preparing the way for a long, deep, mind-blowing kiss. "All I meant was, it's okay to want things for yourself. *Do* things for yourself. I think you've been in survival mode for so long that you've forgotten your dreams."

She sighed. Hoped the tears burning behind her eyes wouldn't find a way to get past her defenses and fall.

How could she tell him that he'd reminded her of all her dreams, brought them back to life with his laughter, his kindness, his intelligence, his lovemaking?

He'd awakened her, not just sexually, but emotionally and even spiritually.

She wasn't going to leave Painted Pony Creek, no matter what, because she knew it was the safest, best place to raise her child.

Jesse, it was clear, had no such plan.

Why had she allowed him to touch her so deeply, to change her so much?

When he left, she would be broken again, and, furthermore, she'd have to hide her disappointment for Isabel's sake. And for her own.

"Come to bed," he said, kissing her forehead.

"Isabel," she said.

"Isabel is asleep," Jesse replied.

"What if she wakes up, and I'm not there?"

"She'll come to our room, looking for you."

Our room. Oh, how Tessa loved those simple, ordinary words.

Even though they weren't true.

Pretending to be angry, she grabbed a sofa pillow and whacked Jesse in the chest with it.

"And exactly what do I say then?" she asked.

Jesse grinned. "You can say I had a nightmare and needed you to keep me company. Any kid would buy that."

"You're awful, Jesse McKettrick."

He rested his forehead against hers, the pillow still wedged between them.

"That isn't what you said last night," he reminded her.

"Stop it," Tessa whispered, blushing, but she didn't want him to stop, and he knew that.

"We'll be quiet," he promised.

Tessa groaned.

"Unlike last night," he added.

With that, he reached over Tessa, switched off the lamp.

"Not here," Tessa rasped.

"Not here," Jesse confirmed.

And then he took her hand, hoisted her onto her feet and pulled her toward the master bedroom.

It was morning, and Isabel was standing in the doorway of Jesse's room, Norvel at her side, staring.

"You had a sleepover," she said, sounding delighted.

Tessa, stark naked under the covers, turned her face into the pillow and groaned. She'd planned to go back to the guest room after she and Jesse had exhausted themselves making slow, silent, fiery love for half the night.

Instead, she'd fallen into a sound, dreamless sleep.

"Yep," Jesse said. "It was a slumber party, actually."

Under the blankets, Tessa jammed one heel into his shin.

He didn't react.

"Norvel needs to go out," Isabel reported.

"Of course he does," Jesse muttered, though his voice was warm, cheerful. "You take him to the back door, and I'll come and let him out."

"Okay," Isabel said, then hurried away, Norvel following.

"A slumber party?" Tessa repeated, face still buried.

She felt Jesse leave the bed, knew he was pulling on a pair of sweatpants, or maybe jeans.

He gave her a teasing swat on the backside. "What was I supposed to say?" he asked, keeping his voice down. "That you couldn't resist having your way with me, even for one night?"

"Shut up," Tessa said, voice muffled.

"I'm letting the dog out," Jesse said, disregarding the suggestion. "After that, I'll shower and get dressed. Take care of the chores. You might want to roll out of your nest and get ready for a big day."

"I don't want to go to town. I don't want to ask if I've still got a job. And I *definitely* don't want to hob-nob with Marjory Bitchface Laughlin."

He swatted her again. "Hostile," he said with a smile in his voice. "We'll take Cruella on together, so don't get all worked up for nothing. Besides, there are other things on the docket—the community Christmas tree lighting, for one."

Tessa groaned. "I need a shower first," she said. "And I don't want to share it, in case you've got any ideas."

"You'd better make it fast, then," he said.

With that, he was gone.

On either side of the icy roads leading into town, the fields glittered like white velvet sprinkled with diamonds, while the trees were silvery pale sketches of themselves, beautiful against the fierce blue of the morning sky.

Tessa, bundled up for the day and wearing one of Jesse's lined denim jackets, allowed the beauty of their surroundings to distract her from the prospect of facing down Marjory Laughlin.

Jesse's presence made her less afraid, but she couldn't help recalling their conversation the night before, when he'd as much as said that he didn't plan to stay in Painted Pony Creek.

Given that she didn't plan to *leave*, there was a problem.

As much joy as she'd found with Jesse, Tessa knew she didn't have another move to another town in her. She loved the Creek, loved that she and Isabel were wanted here, that they were a part of a real community for the first time ever.

Yes, her car was probably bound for the scrap heap, and the little rental house she and Isabel shared was run-down. The pipes rattled. The toilet ran constantly, unless she jiggled the handle. The walls were thin and poorly insulated and the floors sloped. The roof—well, the roof didn't bear thinking about.

Still, she liked the little place and could afford the

rent—barely—and, thanks to the woodstove, she could manage the cost of utilities, though it was always tight.

This morning, Tessa actually dreaded going back to that house, because, due to her lengthy absence, the place would be bitterly cold, not to mention damp and dank, but she didn't want herself or Isabel getting too used to the many comforts of Jesse's borrowed cottage, either.

There was no way she'd ever be able to afford anything remotely comparable.

They were in town, headed for Bailey's, when she dared risk a sidelong glance at Jesse's strong, handsome profile.

God, he was *so far* out of her league. What had she been thinking, getting involved with a man like him?

"I don't know what's going through your mind right now," he said, and his voice startled her because she'd thought his attention was fixed on the road, "but I don't think I'd like it if I did."

"Not now," she said softly. Miserably. Isabel was with them, and well within earshot.

"Right," Jesse replied, and he sounded mildly frustrated.

"Look! They put up a big Santa Claus!" Isabel cried. Sure enough, the hardware-store turkey had already been replaced by another massive display—Santa, his overloaded sleigh, eight not-so-tiny reindeer, and, of course, Rudolph, red nose and all.

Tessa smiled, although she always felt a sort of fretful pressure from signs of Christmas. For Isabel's sake, she made the effort to be cheerful.

"There he is, in all his glory," she said.

"He's waving," Isabel said enthusiastically, waving back.

The corner of Jesse's mouth ticked up, probably because Isabel was so clearly enjoying the moment. "Did you write him a letter yet?" he asked companionably.

"Silly," scoffed Isabel, her little voice piping with affection for this man who included her so easily into his everyday life. "I can't write. I'm only five!"

Jesse chuckled. "I happen to know you can read, missy, so I figured you could probably write, too."

Looking back at her daughter, her heart ready to burst with love and the primal urge to keep this child safe at all costs, Tessa watched as Isabel shook her head vigorously from side to side. "I can write my name," the child said proudly. "I can say my alphabet, too. It's just a matter of time until I can write as well as anybody."

"I'm thinking it'll be about five minutes from now,"

Jesse said, steering the truck into the semi-crowded parking lot beside Bailey's.

Tessa had been enjoying the exchange, even though it gave her a pang of sadness to think such moments as these were as temporary as the weather.

When she turned from watching Isabel, she gasped.

There was a stretch limo in the lot, taking up three spaces.

Such vehicles were, of course, rare in Painted Pony Creek.

This one was empty, and its driver stood beside it, smoking.

The realization left Tessa feeling as though she'd been trampled by a herd of buffalo.

Marjory is inside Bailey's, waiting for me.

Waiting for Isabel.

Not surprisingly, Jesse read Tessa's expression easily.

"Is that Santa Claus's car?" Isabel asked.

"No," Tessa said, setting her jaw so hard that it hurt.

"You can do this, Tessa," Jesse said quietly. "And I'll be with you, every step of the way."

Every instinct urged her to run away—again—but, in the end, she just couldn't do it. What she and Isabel had there in Painted Pony Creek was well worth fighting for, and she intended to stand her ground.

Once parked, Jesse got out, unbuckled Isabel from the booster seat and held her in strong, gentle arms. The way a father held his child.

Tessa squared her shoulders, drew a deep breath.

Then she stormed toward the restaurant, flung open the door and looked around.

Marjory Laughlin rose from her chair at a nearby table. Somewhere in her midsixties, tall and regal, with her dyed platinum blond hair swept up, she moved like a queen passing through a throng of peasants.

Too bad none of them carried torches or pitchforks.

They were watching closely, though, these people Tessa had come to know and like over the past three months.

Odd as it seemed, she felt their silent support.

And Jesse had her back, literally. She knew he was standing just behind her.

"Finally!" Marjory trilled, managing to inject her posh accent even into that one word. "My granddaughter!" Ignoring Tessa, she stepped forward, holding out her arms for Isabel.

Tessa wasn't about to be ignored.

She blocked Marjory's way, arms folded, and the strength in her own voice truly surprised her.

"Do. Not. Touch. My. Child."

"Don't be difficult," Marjory almost sang, doing a credible job of looking and sounding every inch the mistreated, misunderstood grandmother.

"If you touch my daughter," Tessa said, through her teeth, "*I will knock you out.*"

Marjory tsk-tsked. "Come now. There's no need to be so dramatic. You are overreacting, dear."

"Isn't *that* the song of the narcissist," Tessa said, refusing to give so much as the proverbial inch. "If someone calls you on your bullshit, you say they're dramatic. They're overreacting. It's classic."

Marjory looked pained. Her eyes filled with crocodile tears.

Most likely, she was hoping to win the sympathy of the other people in the restaurant, or maybe Jesse's.

Fat chance of that.

"You do realize," he put in quietly, "that there is a restraining order in effect, and you can be jailed for not abiding by it?"

"Nonsense," Marjory said, pulling a lace-trimmed hankie from the sleeve of her formfitting designer dress and dabbing delicately at her eyes. "*Jailed?* For wanting to see my own granddaughter? What is this world coming to?" She paused, looked around, seeking support, finding only grim suspicion.

"She's not your granddaughter," Tessa said.

At last, Marjory gave up the effort to win over the crowd and showed her true disposition. "She is my stepson's child," she said, seething, narrowing her eyes and leaning in until Tessa could feel the woman's coffee-warmed breath on her face. "And that makes her my granddaughter!"

"Brent signed away his rights a long time ago," Tessa said. "And, besides, you're *not* Brent's biological mother, so you have no genetic claim on my daughter."

Tessa felt a rush of cold air behind her, but she didn't look away from Marjory's face.

"Semantics," Marjory said dismissively, peering past Tessa and focusing on Isabel. "Come to Grandmother, sweetheart. You don't have to live in filthy motels or your mother's disreputable car anymore. There's a place for you in one of the finest homes in Boston."

"You're *not* my grandmother," Isabel cried, trembling in Jesse's arms, her little face buried in the collar of his coat. "You're a bad lady and you tried to steal me from my mommy!" Her voice was muffled, but her words were clear. "Go away. Just go away!"

Jesse stepped forward to stand beside Tessa.

Out of the corner of her eye, Tessa saw Alice and

Mike and Miranda all draw closer, soon joined by practically every customer in the restaurant.

"Mommy?" the little girl whimpered.

"I'm here, sweetheart," Tessa replied. "I'm not going
anywhere, and neither are you."

Jesse said nothing, but his grip on Isabel was beyond firm.

Tessa turned, hoping to see Melba or Sheriff Garrett
among the protective crowd.

The person she hadn't expected to see was Brent.

"Mother," he said coldly, addressing his stepmother,
"if you don't let this go, right now, you'll be arrested.
And so help me God, I will *not* bail you out—not unless I've managed to secure a place for you in a psychi-
atric hospital first."

Marjory looked dumbfounded. "You followed me
here?" she asked.

Brent had gained weight since Tessa had seen him
last, and he seemed self-assured, rather than arrogant.
His hair was thinning, and his clothes were as expen-
sive as ever—his black overcoat was definitely cashmere.
Only tailor-made garments were allowed to grace Brent
Laughlin's frame.

"Yes," he replied flatly. "I *did* follow you here. Sheriff Garrett got in touch with me soon after you arrived,

and I came as quickly as I could. He's agreed not to toss you in the hoosegow and press a laundry list of other charges if you leave immediately and agree never to contact Tessa or her daughter again."

Her daughter, Tessa thought. Not his.

Tessa didn't mind that distinction. Brent had no interest whatsoever in Isabel and, as cold and callous as that sounded, she was glad.

She was even a little bit grateful.

After all, he'd come all this way to corral his stepmother. Interrupted his busy, glamorous round of high-profile business meetings and high-maintenance women to make his way to Painted Pony Creek, Montana.

He barely glanced at Isabel, who was still holding on to Jesse for dear life.

Marjory gazed imploringly at Brent. "But Isabel is your only heir!"

Tessa would have bet money that Brent hadn't remembered his daughter's name prior to Marjory's mention of it, but that didn't matter. He was a sperm donor, not a father.

And he was determined to remove the she-devil.

"Hardly," Brent said with an undercurrent of disdain that made Tessa want to kick him, though the desire quickly subsided. "Dad has another family now,

Mother. You know this. He and Ann have two little boys."

Apparently horrified, or wanting to project that, anyway, Marjory gasped and put a hand to her throat in a pearl-clutching gesture.

And she'd called *Tessa* dramatic.

"Those children are *illegitimate*," Marjory nearly growled.

"No, they're not. They're just not connected to you," Brent pointed out. "Now, let's go, Mother, before the sheriff and the chief of police have to flip a coin to see who gets to cuff you and drag you out of here."

Marjory seemed to know she was beaten, but she was all dignity as she collected her long, black coat from the row of hooks beside the door, put it on and stepped outside.

"I apologize, Tessa," Brent said, his gaze moving from her face to Jesse's and back again.

In the next moment, to Tessa's surprise, he reached out a tentative hand as though to touch Isabel, then changed his mind and withdrew it.

"Keep her away from us, Brent. If she bothers Isabel— or me—I promise you, I won't hesitate to press charges. And I'll be keeping the restraining order in place."

"Once, she was a wonderful stepmother," Brent said

discractedly, as though thinking aloud, and as though Tessa hadn't spoken at all. "I was very young when my mother died, and completely lost, and when Marjory came on the scene, things changed for the better. She adopted me and everything. Then, three years ago, Dad walked out on her and remarried. He's had two sons with his new wife, and I guess Mother thought she could maintain some control of Laughlin Enterprises and the family fortune by dragging my illegitimate child into the mess."

Tessa bristled at the word *illegitimate*, though she guessed it was true, but she said nothing. She just wanted this to be over, so she wouldn't have to be afraid for Isabel anymore.

Meanwhile, Brent seemed to come back to himself; he focused a mildly troubled gaze on Tessa and, by extension, Isabel and Jesse.

"Again, Tessa, I'm sorry. I had no idea she was so fixated on you and the child, or I would have done something sooner. I'll personally guarantee you that she'll never bother either of you again."

"How can you promise that?" Tessa wanted to know. "Marjory is clearly unhinged."

"Exactly. I'll be sending her to a private hospital in Switzerland right away. She'll be there for months, perhaps years, if that's what it takes. She'll rest, get her medications adjusted, have some therapy. If all that doesn't straighten her out, I'll let you know—*and* I'll take whatever steps I must to make sure she'll be no trouble to you."

"One text, one email, one *word* from Marjory and I'll fight back, and fight back hard. There will be no holds barred."

Brent smiled sadly. "Mother won't risk being arrested, Tessa. That would destroy her, not only on social media, but among her friend circle, her charity groups, all of it. Trust me on that. After her time-out in Switzerland, she'll have a much better perspective."

Tessa merely nodded, her throat thick with emotion.

Somewhere deep inside her, though, something stirred.

It was hope, she realized. It was a whispered promise that she and Isabel would finally be safe from Marjory Laughlin. Always.

"One last thing," Brent said, rubbing one temple with the tips of his fingers as he turned to go. "Her college fund is intact, but Isabel is no longer in line to inherit the family estate, now that my father has younger sons."

Tessa said nothing. She didn't care about any inheritance.

And so, having said his piece, Brent sighed, then left the restaurant.

Two separate limos drove past the steam-fogged windows of Bailey's and, just like that, it was over.

Everyone in the place clapped, and people returned to their tables and their seats at the counter.

Tessa would be forever grateful to them for their willingness to come to her and Isabel's aid, if that had become necessary.

Isabel, for her part, finally lifted her head from Jesse's shoulder, though she didn't slacken her grip on his neck or make any other move to indicate that she wanted to be put down, to stand on her own.

"Is the mean lady gone?" she asked, probably puzzled by the applause.

"Yes," Tessa said, feeling as though her knees might buckle as all that adrenaline waned like seawater slipping away from the shore. "The mean lady is gone."

"For good, I'm thinking," Melba said with a broad grin.

Eli Garrett, who had just arrived, along with the chief, ironically missing most of the action, smiled, patted Isabel's back. A father himself, his touch was gentle. "That's right," he added.

Tessa wondered what extra charges he'd threatened to press against Marjory, while consulting with Brent earlier, besides harassment and stalking, and then she decided she didn't want to know.

Things settled down considerably.

"Am I fired?" Tessa asked when Alice Bailey came forward to hug her.

"Of course not," Alice replied. She glanced toward the sheriff, who was being welcomed at one of the tables, along with Melba. "My son-in-law is something, isn't he?" she asked proudly. "And did you get a look at Melba's face? She was ready to hog-tie that woman and drag her out of Painted Pony Creek by the hair."

Melba, close enough to overhear, jutted an affirmative thumb into the air.

"Shall I clock in now, or later, in time for the supper crowd?" Tessa asked after tossing the chief an appreciative smile.

"You've had enough excitement for one day," Alice responded. "And so has our girl Isabel. Spend some time reassuring the little one—and don't forget the tree in front of the courthouse will be lit up at sunset." She patted Isabel's cheek. Coaxed a smile from her. "You don't want to miss that," she added mischievously, "since Santa's going to be there, too."

"In person?" Isabel asked.

"In person," Alice replied.

Mike, Alice's stocky, white-haired husband, entered the conversation. "Ho ho ho," he said with a wink.

"Do I get to tell him what I want for Christmas?" Isabel said, brow wrinkled in evident concern. "Or will there be too many other kids there?"

"Tell you what, princess," Mike said. Clearly, given her fondness for wearing her Halloween costume as often as possible, her reputation had preceded her. "You tell me, right now, and I'll pass the word along to Old Saint Nick. We go way back, he and I."

Isabel's eyes widened. She leaned forward, cupped one little hand around Mike's ear and stage-whispered, "I want my own pony, please, and I want my mommy not to be lonesome and scared anymore. Plus, I want a daddy."

Jesse pushed his free hand through his hair.

Mike cleared his throat.

"Let's go home and make sure the pipes haven't burst in all this cold weather," Tessa said, blushing.

"And after that," Jesse put in, "I think we'd better get a Christmas tree."

Isabel let out a delighted squeal and hugged Jesse's neck even harder than before.

Over Isabel's head, his gaze connected with Tessa's.

He didn't even try to hide the fact that his eyes had misted over.

★ ★ ★

The tiny rental house was, as Tessa expected, very cold inside.

Jesse added wood to the living room stove, and soon, a nice fire was blazing away, pushing back the damp chill.

Tessa and Isabel huddled nearby, in anticipation of blessed heat.

Despite feeling shaken from her encounter with Marjory, and then Brent—or maybe because of it—Tessa was feeling a new strength, a new confidence in herself and her ability to look after her child and keep her from harm.

For all her struggles and doubts, she'd finally realized that the *real* Tessa, the one who could stand up to a challenge and not back down, had been with her all along.

"Are we still going to get a Christmas tree?" Isabel asked, shivering inside her coat.

Tessa took her own coat off and draped it over Isabel's. Instead of answering, she glanced at Jesse, who had just returned from checking the small house for any signs of water damage.

"We sure are," he said. "But let's get you warmed up a little first, okay?"

"I'm w-w-warm now," Isabel protested, teeth chattering.

Jesse went to Isabel, removed Tessa's coat and handed it back to its owner, then wrapped his own around the child. "Listen," he said, so gently that Tessa's chin wobbled and she had to look away for a moment. "I promise you we'll go and find a tree, Isabel. Today. And, like your mom—" here, he shifted his gaze to Tessa's face, just for a moment "—I always keep my promises."

Tessa's heart nearly splintered when Isabel, nearly swallowed up by Jesse's coat, burst into tears and, once again, buried her little face in his neck, the way she had at Bailey's during the showdown.

"Hey, kiddo," Jesse said gruffly, patting Isabel's small back with one tentative hand and casting another glance Tessa's way. "Everything's all right now."

"I don't want the bad lady to take me away!" Isabel cried.

Tessa stepped in, and Jesse made room for her. "No one," she told the child, "is *ever* going to take you away, sweetheart. I'll fight like a tiger if they try!"

That seemed to reassure Isabel, at least slightly.

Tessa rescued the child from the heavy coat and led her to the big armchair, where they sat together, Isabel huddled in her mother's embrace.

Without a word, Jesse left the room momentarily and returned with a quilt.

He placed it so carefully over the two of them as Tessa, on the verge of tears herself, hugged her little girl tight and whispered words of comfort and reassurance.

After some time, Isabel settled down; her breathing returned to a more normal rate and she stopped trembling.

In the interim, Jesse had gone into the kitchen, opened and closed cupboards—and, once, the refrigerator door. Finally, the teakettle began to sing its shrill and steaming song.

When he returned to the living room, he carried two mugs, one in each hand. "I couldn't find any marshmallows," he said easily, "and the milk went bad while you were away, so I got rid of that. Fortunately, there was some packaged hot chocolate mix in the pantry, so *voila!*" He set the mugs on the end table beside Tessa's chair, and their gazes met—or, rather, collided.

The impact was cosmic in scope.

She could tell by Jesse's expression that he'd felt it, too.

Isabel, of course, was oblivious. She began to wriggle, wanting out from under the blanket, reminding Tessa of a little flower, shedding petals.

"I'm too *hot*," she informed Tessa.

"Are you all done crying and being scared?" Tessa asked tenderly.

"I think so," replied the child. Isabel needed two things just then, a tissue and a warm washcloth to wipe away the vestiges of her recent meltdown.

Tessa took her daughter to the bathroom, where Isabel was persuaded to blow her nose and submit to a thorough face-washing.

When the two of them returned to the living room, their cups of cocoa and Jesse, the house seemed more hospitable.

Jesse was moving furniture—the two chairs in front of the living room window.

"Will this work?" he asked. "For the tree, I mean?"

Tessa and Isabel agreed with identical nods.

Three hours later, after attending the tree-lighting ceremony at the courthouse, where Santa arrived on the scene in a horse-drawn sleigh, waving cheerily and ho-ho-hoing just like Mike Bailey had, they'd visited one of the town's several Christmas tree farms. There, they'd selected a beauty, six and a half feet of live, lush, fragrant blue spruce.

The tree stood in a pot of soil, ready to be transplanted as soon as the ground softened a little.

Tessa's collection of decorations was modest, given that she and Isabel had been near-constant travelers over the past several years, but once Jesse had strung the lights, and they'd hung the branches with baubles and wilted tinsel, it was as if there had been a magical transformation.

Tessa, the inveterate fan of old movies, was reminded of the scene in *The Bishop's Wife*, when Cary Grant, a visiting angel, had set another Christmas tree aglow with a wave of one celestial hand.

Things like this happened in Painted Pony Creek, Montana, she thought to herself. Wonderful, unexpected, *heart-healing* things.

Tears blurred her vision as she gazed at that tree, watching as Jesse lifted Isabel up high so she could place the treasured, tattered, thrift-store angel on top.

The colors looked smudged, and Tessa would have sworn that, in the space of a heartbeat, the angel fluttered her feathery wings.

❄ **10** ❄

One year later

Jesse rolled over in bed, draping one arm and one leg over Tessa's warm, silken and deliciously naked body. He nuzzled the sensitive place under her ear and whispered, "It's almost Christmas, Mrs. McKettrick. Do you know what I'm asking for this year?"

Tessa, who loved being awakened in just this way, giggled into the softness of her pillow, feeling snug under the heavy quilt. "I think I can guess," she said, rolling over to face him.

He kissed her nose, drew her close. "Oh, yeah?" he teased, his voice throaty. "Go ahead—guess."

She almost told him then, but she managed to restrain herself.

Under their ridiculously large Christmas tree, there was a very special gift tucked behind the other beautiful packages, and she didn't want to spoil the surprise.

Given how intuitive her husband was, Tessa figured he already had a pretty good idea what he was receiving for Christmas that year, their first as a married couple.

Before she could respond, Isabel—accompanied by Norvel, from the sounds of it—could be heard pounding down the long hallway from her bedroom. Upon arrival, she rapped at one of the double doors of the bedroom and called out, "Can we come in?"

"One second," Jesse called back, scrambling into a pair of sweatpants and then sitting down on the edge of the bed. "Okay," he said. "Come in."

Isabel entered. "Daddy," she said in mild reproof. "Why are you and Mommy *still* in bed? Tomorrow's Christmas Eve, and we have to get ready."

Tessa groaned and pulled the covers over her head.

She and Jesse had married six months ago, in mid-June, in the church at Bitter Gulch, and since then, she'd left her job at Bailey's to serve as the Gulch's entertainment and event manager. She loved her work, but it was demanding, and sleeping in of a morning was a rare treat.

Jesse, having completed construction on his brother's brainchild, which was a hit with locals and visitors alike, had spent the last year doing what he loved—building.

Well, that was *one* of the things he loved doing.

He'd purchased 110 acres of land on the other side of Painted Pony Creek from Liam's ranch, after he and Tessa agreed it was just the place for their new home.

Their own small ranch.

They'd conferred endlessly over sketches and blue-prints—these last drawn up by Liam, who had moved to his ranch last spring, just before the official opening of Bitter Gulch—and then the construction had begun.

The new house was U-shaped, built around a central courtyard with a stone fountain, and Tessa had loved it from the first moment she saw its framework walls. The place itself had seemed to embrace her, Isabel and Jesse from the beginning.

It was definitely home, beautifully designed, with a spacious, modern kitchen, living and dining rooms, and no fewer than five bedrooms, each with its own bath.

"Can I step on the button that makes the Christmas tree light up?" Isabel wanted to know. *"Please?"*

"Feel free," Tessa said, giving a careful stretch.

Jesse pulled a T-shirt on over his head and herded a happy Isabel out of the bedroom. "Come on, kiddo," Tessa heard him say. "You can light up the tree, and then we'll get breakfast started, you and me. Okay?"

"*Okay!*" Isabel nearly shouted. "Don't forget, Norvel's hungry, too," she added as they headed for the living room. "And he needs to go outside."

"He's been outside," Jesse replied. "I let him out—and then back in—an hour ago."

"Can I open one present?" Isabel pressed, probably figuring she was on a roll here. "Just one? After all, it's *almost* Christmas!"

"Almost only counts in horseshoes," Jesse said. "Like it or not, Christmas is still two days away."

Isabel gave an exaggerated groan. "That isn't fair!"

Jesse laughed. "Life is a lot of things, short-stuff, but fair isn't one of them."

Listening, Tessa smiled, and her eyes burned a little.

Just a year ago, she and Isabel had been fugitives, nomads, forced to move on to the next place, mere weeks, sometimes days, after they'd arrived.

No time to settle in, make friends, get their bearings.

Painted Pony Creek, Montana, had been different.

It had been, as Isabel aptly put it, "a place for staying."

And that it was.

Tessa thought the town was enchanted. Here, she'd found security and friendship for herself and her daughter and, best of all, the man she'd been born to love and be loved by—Jesse. They'd taken their time getting to know each other, though Jesse had proposed on the previous Valentine's Day.

That had been a romantic experience; they'd visited the saloon at Bitter Gulch after a private and very sumptuous dinner next door in the hotel kitchen.

There, Jesse had lifted Tessa to sit on the edge of the bar, pulled a small velvet box from the pocket of his jacket and drawled, "Dance-hall gal, will you marry me?"

She'd laughed and cried, both at the same time, flung her arms around Jesse's neck and whispered, "Yes, I will, Marshal McKettrick. Oh, *yes, I will!*"

Once they were married, he'd adopted Isabel, with the child's approval as well as Tessa's, and now the three of them shared the McKettrick name, a sort of intangible seal that made them a family.

Her heart light, Tessa drew a deep breath, threw back the covers and got out of bed.

She went into the master bathroom, a huge space with a garden tub, a shower big enough to accommodate a football team, a double vanity with matching sinks, and bright brass fixtures on everything.

Tessa showered, dried herself off, and dressed in black jeans and a royal blue cashmere sweater, adding a pair of short black boots for good measure. Then she brushed her damp, shoulder-length brown hair back from her face and fastened it into a ponytail.

As she passed through the living room, she paused to admire the spectacular Christmas tree, shining brightly in front of the floor-to-ceiling picture window.

Some of the decorations were the ones that had been carefully and lovingly packed and transported from place to place during Tessa and Isabel's travels. They were traditional in style, shiny glass balls in all colors, old-fashioned bubble lights. There was even tinsel. The stuff made a mess, it was true, but it added something special to the display.

Presents were piled beneath the tree, and the sight of them made Tessa smile and shake her head. Jesse had been stashing away bags and boxes since Thanksgiving; Christmas was a big deal in the McKettrick family, as it turned out, and Jesse was carrying on the tradition.

Cooking sounds floated in from the kitchen, and Jesse and Isabel were chatting away about the event of the day—the big community gathering to be held at Bitter Gulch.

Colored lights had been strung on every building, including the saloon, and Liam had brought in an enormous living Christmas tree—so large that it had been transported by semitruck and set in place in front of the general store by a forklift.

Tessa and her small crew of Christmas elves had spent many chilly but happy hours decorating it, though Liam had insisted on doing the ladder-work on his own.

In the end, Jesse had helped, setting the three-foot-wide golden star on the very top, with Tessa holding her breath the whole time, terrified that he'd fall.

Painted Pony Creek's official tree, in front of the courthouse, had been lit as always, at sunset on the day after Thanksgiving.

Liam hadn't wanted to step on the community's toes by competing, which was why the tree at Bitter Gulch would be set alight this evening, on what Jesse called "Christmas Eve Eve."

Tonight, there would be free admission to Bitter Gulch, along with candy apples, peppermint sticks and three kinds of hot chocolate, as well as coffee and tea. And small gifts, things Tessa herself had selected with great care, for the children and two busloads of nursing home residents, one group from a facility in Painted Pony Creek and another from a similar one in nearby Silver Hills.

Children ten and under were eligible and would receive miniature action figures, while the senior citizens would be given either boxes of chocolate or large-print books.

Tessa stepped into the kitchen, crossed to the counter and poured herself a large mug of hot, fresh coffee.

"Daddy says I can help feed the horses this morning," Isabel chirped. She was standing on a chair with an apron tied around her small torso. She was stirring a huge bowl of what appeared to be pancake batter, and getting a lot of it on herself—and the floor, where Norvel was busy slurping it up.

So much for the no-people-food rule, Tessa thought wryly.

Jesse must have read her expression, if not her mind, because after glancing downward once, he said, "Hey. It's almost Christmas."

Tessa chuckled. "Softy," she said.

Jesse raised one eyebrow, but said nothing, because there was no need.

Isabel, meanwhile, prattled on, so full of anticipation that she could barely stand still. "He shoveled a path from here to the barn last night, so I won't get lost in the snow."

"Well," Tessa observed, leaning against the counter and smiling at Jesse over the rim of her coffee cup. "That's a relief."

"I'll wear my red hat, just in case," Isabel added seriously. "Then, even if you and Daddy couldn't see me, you'd see my red hat!"

"Flawless reasoning," Jesse said, gently taking the wooden spoon from Isabel's hand and lifting her down from the chair. "I'll take it from here," he added.

Jesse was, among his other stellar qualities, a very competent cook.

Soon, the three of them were seated at the round table in the breakfast alcove, scarfing up bacon, eggs and pancakes.

In that space, there were windows on three sides. The snow was still coming down.

Tessa's thoughts slipped briefly to last year's storm, at Thanksgiving. She'd essentially been stranded, since the snow was absolutely relentless, and even though she'd known she cared for Jesse then, and welcomed his lovemaking, she *hadn't* expected to share a future with him.

Hadn't known she would be free of Marjory Laughlin and her obsession with Isabel for good, either.

Thank God she was. Melba, in her capacity as chief of police, had kept an eye on Marjory's doings, mostly via the internet, and informed Tessa that the older woman had benefited from her time in that Swiss sanitarium. She'd married one of her doctors and taken up residence in a grand château in a village at the foot of the Alps.

Did this mean that life would be all sunshine and roses from now on?

Of course not, but Tessa believed in taking one day at a time, in being grateful for every happiness, large or small, and celebrating the best gift life had to offer: true love.

For her, that was enough.

Once breakfast was over, Tessa stayed behind to do the dishes and tidy the kitchen, while Jesse and Isabel bundled up in boots and heavy coats and set out, with Norvel prancing at their heels, for the barn.

When the pair returned, they all headed for town.

The streets there were freshly plowed and sanded, but crowded as well.

Shoppers were out in force, coming in and out of the stores, stopping to chat with friends and neighbors on the salted sidewalks.

Lights were strung across the streets, and every lamp-post boasted greenery set off by twigs of holly, with their bright red berries.

Display windows shimmered with tinsel garlands, and the familiar inflatable Santa and crew bobbed and wobbled on top of the hardware store.

It all looked like a scene from an old-fashioned Christmas card.

Jesse reached over, as if sensing her thoughts—or sharing them, as he often did—and squeezed her hand.

When they arrived at Bitter Gulch, at the far end of the Creek, Liam appeared to let them through the gate. The attraction was closed until two o'clock, when the celebration would begin.

A tall man, lean and muscular, like Jesse, Liam McKettrick had dark hair, just brushing his collar, and his eyes were as blue as indigo or new denim. His smile, again, like his brother's, was a force of nature all by itself.

Tessa liked her brother-in-law, though she often felt sad for him.

Despite all efforts to present a jovial face to the world, she knew he was a lonely man. He'd lost his wife, and his children were still living with their grandparents in Seattle; the kids liked their school and were reluctant to leave their friends.

So far, Liam's young son and daughter hadn't visited him at the ranch except once—when he wanted to see them, he used FaceTime. Sometimes—though not very often—he went to Seattle.

There was a deep sadness lingering behind those too-blue eyes, even when he was flashing that quick, white and very disarming smile of his.

Facing his elder brother on the snowy street, Jesse chuckled, taking in the clothes Liam wore—the plain black trousers and fitted topcoat and rough-and-ready boots. A silver star shone on his lapel, and a holstered pistol—a prop, not a real gun—rode his hip.

"You're taking this Old West thing pretty seriously," Jesse remarked.

The smile returned, but it didn't spark in Liam's eyes. He took in Jesse's newish jeans, polished boots and fleece-lined coat. "And you aren't," he pointed out reasonably.

Jesse ignored that. "You look good, big brother. I could almost forget you're really an architect."

Liam laughed, gestured toward the hotel where employees were mingling, some of them in modern clothes, some in the costumes they wore to entertain the crowds. "Let's get this show on the road, such as it is," he said, as Isabel tugged at his coat sleeve. Without hesitation, he swept the little girl up into his arms. "You ready for a Christmas shindig, little partner?" he asked her.

"Are there presents?" Isabel countered.

"Isabel!" Tessa scolded.

Liam raised a hand to her, though he never looked away from Isabel's shining face. "For you," he said, "yes, there are."

The company Christmas party, a luncheon served in the hotel dining room, was a sparkling bustle of movement and color and laughter and, yes, presents.

All the employees, including Tessa, received hefty bonuses.

The children in attendance were given a choice between radio-operated cars and airplanes and beautifully dressed dolls. Some of the girls chose a car or an airplane, but the boys went with cars and airplanes, every one.

Isabel, innately feminine from birth, picked a doll.

She named her Clarissa on the spot, and refused to be separated from her throughout the party *and* the events of the evening as well.

On the return trip to the ranch, late that night, she clutched the lovely doll in both arms, even as she slept, exhausted, in her booster chair.

Jesse carried his daughter—and her doll—into the house, while Tessa greeted a very happy Norvel and took him outside for a potty break.

Back inside, she found Jesse beside the dark, shimmering tree. He tapped the button on the floor with one foot, and the whole thing gleamed like a colorful starburst in the darkest depths of space.

"She's in her room," he explained, though Tessa hadn't asked about Isabel. They often held conversations like this, with no segues. "I don't think I'm man enough to pry that doll out of her arms."

Tessa crossed the room, stood on tiptoe to kiss her husband's sexy mouth.

"You're man enough for anything," she whispered. "*More* than man enough."

He rested his hands on her hips, gazed down at her. "You're only saying that because you're madly in love with me," he teased.

"I'm madly, truly, deeply in love with you, Jesse McKettrick." They exchanged a soft, nibbling kiss. "And you're all the man I could ever need."

He sighed.

She pushed away from him, but reluctantly. "Isabel," she reminded him.

In Isabel's spacious, girlie room, with its ruffled can-

opy bed, its little-girl dressers, its many stuffed animals
and books and art supplies, Tessa was struck to the heart
by the sight of her sleeping child, still clad in everything but her snow boots, sleeping peacefully atop her
pink chenille bedspread.

We've come so far, you and I, she told her daughter silently. *So far.*

After blinking away more tears—they'd been a regular occurrence recently—Tessa made her way to Isabel's
bedside. She undressed her, wrangled her into pajamas,
and even got her up to use the bathroom and brush her
teeth, though the child was half-asleep the whole time.

She'd been persuaded, with no little difficulty, to
let Clarissa sleep, since she'd undoubtedly had a very
long day.

"Clarissa?" Jesse queried with some amusement when
Tessa joined him on the living room couch before a
crackling fire on the hearth.

The room was dark, except for the fire and the tree.

Tessa knew he was asking why Isabel had chosen
a relatively old-fashioned name for her new doll. It
seemed to her that, sometimes, they read each other's
minds.

She gave little shrug. "Isabel," she said, "is Isabel.

She must have heard the name somewhere and decided she liked it."

Jesse grinned, shook his head. "She's an amazing kid," he said.

She smiled, traced the side of his face with a light index finger. "I love you," she said.

He kissed her briefly. "And I love you," he replied.

They'd often exchanged those words over the past year, but each time they did, they seemed a touch truer than the last time they'd been spoken.

"Do you think Liam is unhappy?" she asked, resting her head against Jesse's shoulder.

"He's very unhappy," Jesse said with regret. "But he'll find his way sooner or later. He always does."

"It makes me sad," Tessa replied.

"Me, too," Jesse answered. "But, hey, it's Christmas Eve Eve, Tess. Let's try to cheer up a little here."

She laughed, fake punched him in the chest. "Were you one of those little kids who sneak out to the tree in the middle of the night and snoop through the presents?" she asked.

"Yes," he admitted. "Liam and Rhett were just as devious, though."

"Did you get caught?" Tessa asked, enjoying the

mental picture of three little boys in pajamas, scoping out Christmas loot in the dark.

"Every time," Jesse said with a chuckle. "What was it like for you?"

The moment the words were out of Jesse's mouth, it was obvious that he regretted them. He'd remembered, too late, that Tessa's childhood had been very different from his.

"I'm sorry," he said.

"Don't be," she said. "I didn't get a lot of presents, but I got enough. Christmas was a happy time for me, like it was for you."

"I didn't mean—"

She kissed him. "Don't apologize," she said. "I've dealt with all that. Besides, it's now that matters, isn't it? And now happens to be pretty darned fabulous."

He freed her hair from its ponytail, kissed her neck.

"Pretty darned fabulous," he agreed.

It snowed the next day, and Isabel was bursting with energy and excitement, so, after breakfast, Jesse took her out to the barn, ostensibly to help feed the horses.

Tessa and Norvel followed, Tessa trying hard to look as though it was an ordinary day, with ordinary chores to be done.

Only, it wasn't.

There was a small, black pony in the first stall. His name had not been selected yet—*anything but Clarissa*, Jesse had joked—but there he was, in the McKettrick barn, occupying his very own stall.

Three of the pony's feet were snow-white, and there was a matching blaze on his face.

Isabel gasped when she saw him through the rails of the stall door, and she started climbing.

Jesse laughed and caught her, lifting her down. "Wait a minute, Annie Oakley. You and your new friend need a little time to get to know each other, don't you think? And what have I told you about climbing into stalls?"

Isabel sighed expansively. "I *wasn't* climbing into his stall," she said. "I just want to pet him."

The pony, and the process of getting to know him, took most of that snowy, glistening day.

By suppertime, Isabel had christened him Midnight and ridden him around and around the pasture, with close supervision from Jesse.

After they'd eaten the evening meal, and all the chores were done, it was time for Isabel to hang her stocking from a hook on the fireplace mantel. There was a second stocking, for Norvel.

Isabel was wired, and Jesse and Tessa took turns read-

ing to her until she finally gave up and allowed herself
to be tucked in for the night. Clutching Clarissa, she
said her prayers and fell into a sound sleep before she
reached "amen."

Following an interlude of quiet talk, when they were
certain Isabel would not come charging out of her bedroom, Jesse brought the "Santa Claus" presents from
their hiding place and set them in the middle of the living room floor, while Tessa, on her hands and knees,
rummaged for the package she'd hidden days before.

It was about eight inches square, and Tessa had
wrapped it in silver paper, tied with a red ribbon and
a simple bow.

Rising to her feet, she held it out to Jesse. "Open it,"
she said very softly.

He studied her face for a moment, then untied the
ribbon, carefully tore away the paper.

Inside was a shoebox, and inside the shoebox was
the tiniest pair of Western boots Tessa had been able
to find.

They were yellow, and thus suitably noncommittal.

Jesse looked puzzled for a moment or so, but then
he stared at her, his face full of hope and cautious joy.
"Tess...?"

"Yes," she told him gently, her own eyes glistening

with tears—again. "Around the middle of June, there'll be a new little ranch hand joining us."

Jesse seemed unable to move or speak, but when he finally managed, he took Tessa into his arms and kissed her.

It was a celebration, that kiss.

Complete with invisible fireworks.

★ ★ ★ ★ ★

Please turn the page for a sneak peek at a brand-new book from #1 New York Times *bestselling author Linda Lael Miller.*

After a disastrous attempt at marriage, Madison Bettencourt returns home to Painted Pony Creek to care for her ailing grandmother and winds up confronting the mystery of what happened to her childhood best friend and unexpectedly finding love.

Enjoy this excerpt from Where the Creek Bends, *Linda Lael Miller's new book available in spring 2024!*

❄ 1 ❄

She burst—no, *erupted*—through a shimmering splash of sunshine, like a human bullet, or an angel stepping in from a neighboring realm where magic was the rule rather than the rare exception.

Half blinded by the glare—it was mid-July, the Montana sky was sugar-bowl blue, and he was sweating in his town-marshal getup—Liam McKettrick squinted hard, sure he was seeing things.

Too much stress, too little sleep.

But she was real.

A bride, in full regalia, veil billowing, lacy skirts and snow-white train trailing in the dry dust of Bitter Gulch's Main Street, was heading straight for the Hard Luck Saloon.

Liam, standing on the balcony outside the make-believe brothel above the very authentic—and currently empty—establishment below, bolted for the back stairs.

Whatever was going on here, he damn well wasn't about to miss it.

He'd just entered the saloon and established himself behind the long bar, idly wiping out a glass with a piece of cloth, when she arrived.

She struck the classic swinging doors with both palms and enough force to send them crashing against the inside wall, then stomped across the sawdust floor to the bar.

After hoisting her slender self onto a stool, she threw back her veil, blew a strand of brown-gold hair off her forehead with one determined breath and slapped one hand down onto the polished surface between them.

"Set 'em up, bartender," she said.

Liam was doing his damnedest not to grin.

The whole thing was bizarre.

And way more fun than he'd ever expected to have on an ordinary day in the "town" of Bitter Gulch—an oasis of fantasy, a place where men, women and children came to escape the modern world for a while and experience the Old West.

Standing at the southern edge of Painted Pony Creek,

Montana, Bitter Gulch was Liam's brainchild; he'd designed it. Hired his younger brother, Jesse, to oversee the construction phase.

Liam swallowed, unable to look away from the bride, especially now that she was up close and very personal. Just across the bar.

She smelled of dust, subtle perfume and something sugary.

"What'll it be?" he asked, his voice slightly hoarse. He didn't use it much, his voice, as a general rule, and it was only eleven o'clock in the morning, according to the huge antique clock on the opposite wall.

So his social skills were still resurfacing.

She paused to ponder the question, looking solemn. She had wide hazel eyes, heavily lashed and full of— something. Indignation, clearly, and confusion.

Pain, too, though she was doing a fairly good job of hiding that.

Liam's heart, usually heavily defended—like an isolated cavalry fort in those thrilling days of yesteryear, besieged by furious warriors riding painted ponies— hitched, and hitched hard.

"Whiskey," the woman decided.

"What kind?" Whiskey was whiskey, and he could

have poured a shot without asking another question, but he wanted to extend this encounter.

It was amazing.

She was amazing, with those expressive eyes. Her skin was flawless, her lips full, and her shining brown hair now slightly out of kilter under the exquisitely made veil, a lacy affair that might have been assembled from starlight and spiderwebs in some strange and secret place beyond the tattered edges of the ordinary world.

"Any kind," she responded.

Liam nodded, put his hand out and introduced himself. "Liam McKettrick," he said.

They shook. Her hand felt dainty, but strong, too.

"Madison Bettencourt," she replied, straightening her spine and lifting her chin a little. Tears rose along her lower lashes and smudged her mascara when she brushed them away with the back of one hand. "By now, I would have been Madison *Sterne*," she told him. "But I bolted."

Liam poured two fingers of Maker's Mark into a clean glass, listening not just with his ears, but with the whole of his being.

It was an unusual thing, the way his senses seemed to be revving up, as if he were a race car instead of a man.

He'd never felt anything quite like this before.

"Ice?" he asked. He pushed the glass toward her, slid it, more like. He wasn't planning on making any sudden moves, lest she dissolve into sparkling particles and disappear. "Maybe some cola?"

Madison glanced back at the double doors, looking a little uneasy. "Ice," she said resolutely. "Otherwise, I'll take it straight."

Again, Liam wanted to laugh, but he knew that would be a mistake.

He filled a paper cup at the ice machine, brought it to Madison without another word.

"Is this place real?" she asked, after dumping the ice unceremoniously into her glass, causing some of it to splash over the rim and stand melting on the scarred wooden surface of the bar.

"What do you mean, is it real?" Liam asked, amused, and not completely able to hide it, try though he did.

"It's like going back in time or something," Madison responded after a long sip of whiskey and an almost comical sigh of satisfaction. "One minute, I was at *my wedding*, across the road, finding out I'd just said 'I do' to a total pushover of a mama's boy, and the next—" She paused, raised and lowered her shoulders in a semi-shrug, and gazed sadly down into her drink.

A moment later, the lovely shoulders slumped slightly,

and the sight gave Liam a twinge deep in his chest. If he'd known her for more than five minutes, he would have put his arms around her right then and there, held her close. Reassured her somehow.

Yet another bad idea.

A few seconds of silence stumbled by. Then she looked up, met his eyes and finished with "The next minute, I was here, in the Old West. In a real saloon." Another sigh. "You know what I wish, Liam Mc-Kettrick the bartender? I wish I really could go back in time. Be somebody else. Live a different life—an entirely different life."

Madison took another swig of her whiskey. At this rate, she was going to be disastrously drunk, and soon.

Liam moved the bottle out of sight and leaned against the bar, bracing himself with his forearms.

She looked him over, taking in his collarless white cotton shirt, the black waistcoat he always wore when he spent time in Bitter Gulch. Along with his tall scuffed boots, suspenders and itchy woolen trousers—not to mention the shiny silver star pinned to his coat—the outfit added to the ambience.

And Bitter Gulch was all *about* ambience.

That was the point of the exercise.

Tourists came from all over the world to don costumes, live the Old West experience. Movies were filmed there on occasion, along with TV series for all the major players in the streaming game.

Liam knew most of the visitors wouldn't have lasted a day in the *real* Old West, but then, that didn't matter. They were paying to pretend, not to teleport themselves back to a previous century, when most of the amenities they were used to had yet to exist. Hot and cold running water had been a rarity in communities like Painted Pony Creek, electricity a fledgling science, and Wi-Fi—well, nonexistent, of course.

He pictured his kids, Keely, nine, and Cavan, seven, riding in wagons or on horseback everywhere they went, stripped of their cell phones, their tablets, the huge flat-screen TV in their grandparents' family room, and smiled.

God, he missed them.

"You wouldn't like it," he responded at some length. He'd gotten lost in those lovely eyes of hers, along with his own thoughts.

"I wouldn't like what?" she asked, still putting on a brave front.

"Life in the past," he replied. "There are reasons why we're advised to live in the present, you know."

She let the remark pass.

"Are you really a lawman?" Madison inquired, having drained her glass while Liam was pondering the situation and, as always, wishing Keely and Cavan were with him instead of far away, staying with their grandparents in Seattle.

Liam allowed himself a minimal grin, really just an uptick at one corner of his mouth, hardly noticeable to the casual observer. "No," he replied. "I'm an architect."

Madison frowned, musing again. She was getting tipsy, and Liam wondered how much champagne she'd had before deciding to ditch the mama's boy.

What a numbskull that guy must be.

"You don't look like an architect," she responded solemnly.

"What does an architect look like?" he asked.

"I don't know," Madison answered, still as serious as the proverbial heart attack. "But I'd have pegged you for an actor, with your dark hair and those indigo-blue eyes and—well." She paused, gestured with both hands, indicating their surroundings. "When I picture an architect, I guess I see someone more—ordinary. Like an accountant."

"An accountant," Liam echoed, hiding another grin.

"Whatever," Madison said, and now she sounded

cheerier, although the word got tangled up in her tongue before she turned it loose.

Resolutely, she slapped the bar again. "More whiskey."

"Look," Liam reasoned. "Maybe it isn't the best idea—"

"Are you cutting me off?" she interrupted, though calmly. Her beautifully shaped eyebrows drew together for a moment.

"No," Liam replied. "I'm just suggesting that, after what happened today, you might want to pace yourself a bit. That's all."

"Do you want to know, Liam McKettrick, architect and barkeep, just what *did* happen? I mean, bartenders are supposed to be good listeners, right?"

"I'd say I'm a pretty fair listener," Liam allowed. Then, knowing he'd already lost the argument, unspoken though it was, he picked up the bottle he'd set aside moments before, twisted off the cap and poured her a double.

"I could use one of those right about now," Madison replied after another healthy swig of liquor. "A good listener, I mean."

"Okay, shoot," Liam said. He'd done a lot of listening in his life, largely because he was, as the saying

went, a man of few words. So many people were uncomfortable with silence, felt a need to speak into it.
"What happened?"

Madison mirrored his earlier posture, leaning on her
forearms, all but hidden by puffy sleeves, and said in a
confidential tone, "You won't believe it."

"Try me," Liam urged. Standing back a little, to give
the runaway bride some space. No sense crowding her.

She seemed solid, but magical, too, which meant
she could be a figment of his imagination, not a regular woman.

"I really thought Jeffrey was the man for me," she
began, shaking her head, apparently reflecting upon
her previous choices. "I mean, he was so different from
my first husband. Tom was a lying, cheating dirtbag."

Liam raised one eyebrow, though he was pretty sure
she didn't notice that. She was too involved in the story
she was telling.

"Your first husband?" he prompted casually, picking
up the cloth, wiping down the spotless surface of the
bar, glancing at the clock again. In less than an hour,
Bitter Gulch would be open for business, bustling with
appropriately costumed employees and the usual horde
of families on summer vacation.

This delightful interlude would be over.

And how many times could something like this happen in one man's life?

"Yes," she began. "His name was—is—Tom Wainwright. He's an airline pilot, very good-looking and very macho. We were married for three years."

Liam thought of his own marital history. Reminded himself he was in no position to judge, given that he'd gone into that crap show of a marriage with both eyes wide-open.

His late wife, Waverly, a model and sometime actress, had been beautiful, with her fit, slender body, her gleaming dark hair, her stunning green eyes.

She'd also been a walking red flag, vindictive when she was angry, which was often, jealous of just about everybody, and prone to straying, although Liam hadn't known that until he was in way over his head, with two children to think about.

Inwardly, he sighed. "Go on," he said.

Madison's fascinating chameleon eyes seemed to be fixed on another place and time. "He promised," she said.

Liam waited.

"Tom knew I wanted children more than anything, and he promised we would start a family as soon as he got promoted, after we moved, that kind of thing. And, like a fool, I believed him." Madison paused, looked down at her drink. Her left hand, shimmering with a doorknob of a diamond and an impressive wedding band to match, trembled slightly. "Turns out, he never wanted children. He was just stringing me along, waiting for my grandmother to die, so he could raid my inheritance. And if all that wasn't bad enough, he got another woman pregnant. I divorced him."

"Understandable," Liam said, not wanting to break the flow. He felt honored, somehow, receiving her confidences in that quiet and otherwise empty saloon.

And very sympathetic. After all, he could identify. He would have divorced Waverly, for similar reasons, if she hadn't gotten sick. She'd died only six months after she'd been diagnosed with a virulent strain of leukemia.

Everything he'd felt for her had dried up and blown away like so much dust once he'd finally admitted to himself that she'd been unfaithful, not just once or twice, but dozens of times.

But she'd been so desperately ill.

And she *was* the mother of his children.

He'd had to stand by her, whether he wanted to or not.

And stand by her he had, until the end, though even as she was dying, Waverly had been distant with him, cold.

If it weren't for you and these kids, she'd said once, lying skeletal in her hospital bed, breathless and bitter, while machines beeped and wheezed around her, *I would have been famous. I would have been somebody special.*

The memory, brief as it was, caused Liam to shut his eyes for a moment.

When he opened them again, Madison was throwing back more whiskey.

She teetered a little on the stool in the process, and Liam reached for her, caught himself just short of grabbing her forearm to keep her from falling right into the sawdust.

"So that was that, with Tom at least," she went on, sounding resigned. "I met Jeffrey a year later—I think I mentioned that he's an accountant—and he really fits the stereotype of the nerdy guy who's more interested in numbers than people…and—"

She fell silent again. Staring down at her drink, probably fighting back tears.

Liam had never longed to put his arms around a woman the way he did then, but that was a risk he didn't want to take.

She might vanish.

Anyway, somebody was bound to come looking for her soon—the nerd groom, for example, or her mother.

It was a wonder no one had tracked her down yet, in fact, since Brynne Garrett's fancy wedding venue was just on the other side of the road.

He'd noticed the crowd gathered around the flower-draped gazebo earlier, though it wasn't an unusual sight, since Brynne and her business partner, David Fielding, did a land-office business throwing lavish weddings, many of them complete with fireworks, strange costumes and paid extras.

Now he imagined the drama and chaos that must have started when the bride turned her "I do" into an "I don't" and fled the scene in a fist-clenching fury.

Again, he allowed himself the faintest of grins, savoring the memory of her spectacular arrival, a creature of light and flame and sweet, sweet frenzy.

"And today, you married Jeffrey," he ventured to get the conversation moving again.

"Sort of," she said, with another sigh and another swirl and another swig.

More like a gulp.

"How do you 'sort of' get married?"

"I went through with the ceremony," she recalled. "We exchanged vows in front of that lovely gazebo, and the minister pronounced us husband and wife. We went into the lodge then, since it was time for the reception to start. Jeffrey's mother sidled up to me, all smiles, and said she was so thrilled to be going on the honeymoon with us. Turned out, Jeffrey had bought her an airline ticket, behind my back, and even reserved a room for her at our hotel."

"Uh-oh," Liam muttered with conviction. In any other circumstances, he would have added a whistle for emphasis.

"I'm such a fool!" Madison lamented. "Jeffrey actually invited *his mother* to join us *on our honeymoon*, and I didn't see it coming. I should have, because there were plenty of warning signs, but I didn't!"

Liam was sympathetic—and fascinated. "What happened then?"

"I confronted Jeffrey and he admitted it was true. His mommy needed a vacation, and she'd always wanted to visit Costa Rica. Can you believe it?"

Liam was stuck for an answer, so he didn't offer one.

"I told Jeffrey we were through, this time for good, and I refused to sign the license, which meant we weren't legally married. We'd been through the motions, but none of it was binding.

"He got really upset and said I was just being selfish and overdramatic. I told him he and his mother both needed therapy, and turned to leave. He grabbed my arm, trying to stop me, I guess, and when he did that, I completely lost it. I whirled on him, ready to pop him one, right in the mug. I didn't, but he stumbled backward anyway, lost his footing and fell into the cake."

Liam was really enjoying the scenes unrolling in his head. It was like something out of a movie.

Madison seemed almost cheerful now, even smiling a little as she recalled the encounter. "His mother— *Yolanda*—tried to help him up. She slipped in the frosting and scattered cake on the floor and fell on top of him. They were both squirming around in the goop, trying to get back on their feet, when I left."

"I take it this wasn't the first time Jeffrey's mother had been a problem?"

Madison drew a deep breath, causing her perfect breasts to rise beneath the silk and lace of her bodice, and exhaled loudly, in obvious frustration.

Remembering, she shook her head. "That woman— Yolanda, I mean—was always interfering. She was awful, actually. Always passive-aggressive—with *me*, that is. Clingy and possessive, too, forever fawning over Jeffrey, calling him her baby boy." She paused, shook her head. "I'm such a ninny."

"You don't strike me as a ninny," Liam observed moderately, wondering how long it had been since he'd heard that old-fashioned term. "Maybe you're being a little too hard on yourself?"

"Kind of you to say so," Madison said, softly and sadly. "But I have to take full responsibility. I wanted an ordinary man—somebody solid and dependable—not an overgrown jock like Tom. I thought Jeffrey was that man, and he said he wanted children, so I guess I was willing to overlook some of his faults—after all, I'm not exactly perfect myself."

Liam figured that was debatable, but he didn't say so. That would have been flattery, and he didn't deal in that.

"The signs were there all along," Madison continued quietly, reflectively. "Yolanda was around way too much. She went to movies with us, for heaven's sake, and crashed more than one otherwise romantic dinner. We took a day trip to the beach once, and she followed us there."

"Wow," Liam said, because speaking his thoughts about Jeffrey's relationship with his mother would have been rude. Plus, it was none of his business.

Madison fixed her gaze on him in the next moment, eyes slightly narrowed, brows raised. "What's *your* mother like?" she asked forthrightly.

The question took Liam aback, unexpected as it was.

"Different," he said after a few long moments. "From Yolanda, that is."

"She doesn't interfere in your life? Invite herself along on your dates?"

"God, no," Liam said, trying to picture his independent mother behaving the way this Yolanda person apparently did. Cassie McKettrick loved her children, for sure, and she had been an active, attentive parent when they were young, making sure they led happy lives and behaved themselves. For all that, she had always been more than a mother, more than a wife.

She was an artist, a businesswoman, a thriving entity in her own right.

Now that all three of them were grown men, he, Jesse and Rhett, the youngest, Cassie was too busy sculpting museum-quality pieces, helping run the family's sizable ranch in Southern California and serving on various charity boards to be overly concerned with what might be happening in the lives of her sons.

The faintest blush pinkened Madison's cheeks. "I'm sorry. I shouldn't have asked such personal questions."

"Don't be sorry," Liam said. He could hear car doors slamming now, female voices rising and falling, drawing nearer.

It was over, this odd encounter, and Liam wanted it to last longer. A *lot* longer.

"That will be my friends," Madison said, draining the last drops of whiskey and melted ice with an obvious swallow.

She was right, of course.

There were footsteps on the wooden sidewalk out front, and some of the chatter was discernible now.

"I'm sure she's here somewhere," a woman said.

"I saw her heading this way," said another.

"I wouldn't blame her for taking to drink," offered still another.

And then the saloon doors opened again, and four women in voluminous gowns of pale pastels—pink, blue, green and yellow—surged inside all at once, good-naturedly colliding with each other as they came.

"There you are, Mads!" cried the blonde in pink.

"We were worried about you," chided the brunette in blue.

"Big-time," confirmed the redhead in green.

The last of the company, dressed in yellow, wore a turban, and apparently had nothing to add to the conversation.

"Is he gone?" Madison asked, turning slightly to look

back at the gaggle of probable bridesmaids, given the way they were dressed.

She was just as beautiful in profile.

"Gone?" the blonde echoed, pink skirts swishing as she crossed the sawdust floor to touch Madison's shoulder gently. "For now, yes. He left the venue right after the cake incident, with Mommy tripping solici-tously along behind him, tsk-tsking all the way." She laughed, and Liam decided he liked her. "I suppose they're probably at the hotel by now, recovering from the humiliation."

The brunette giggled and did a little dance. "Mads," she said, "this was absolutely *the best* wedding I've ever been to!"

"It was a disaster," Madison reminded them, some-what dryly.

"Social media gold," objected the redhead. "By now, videos of Jeffrey and his mother squirming around in all that cake goop are bouncing off satellites and land-ing on phone screens all over the world!"

"Who's this?" purred the one in the yellow turban, giving Liam the once-over.

"This," Madison said with an exaggerated gesture of one hand, "is Liam McKettrick, the listening bartender/architect/town marshal."

He inclined his head slightly, in an unspoken "hello."

"Liam," Madison went on expansively, "meet my best friends—"

She reeled off their names, rapid-fire. Not one of them stuck in Liam's brain.

"I think it's time we got you home," the blonde—Alisa, Ariel, Annette?—said, turning her attention back to her friend, the runaway bride. "You need to get out of that dress, have something to eat—"

"And sober up," put in the redhead.

"Home?" Madison ruminated. She was definitely drunk. "And where is that, exactly?"

The blonde poked an arm through Madison's and helped her off the bar stool.

The almost bride hesitated, frowned. "Wait. I didn't pay for my drink!"

"On the house," Liam said.

"Thanks," said the blonde with a brief glance his way.

With that, having surrounded her, the group maneuvered Madison toward the doors.

Liam followed, at a little distance, amused by the colorful birdlike bevy of women, all of them talking at once.

It took some doing to get through the swinging

doors, since walking single file evidently hadn't occurred to them.

They navigated the wide sidewalk, still in a cluster, then made their communal way around the hitching rail and water trough directly in front of the saloon.

Liam leaned against one of the poles supporting the narrow roof above the entrance, watching them all, trundling toward a white compact car waiting in the road.

Nothing would ever top the sight of Madison Bettencourt storming into the saloon in that grand gown of hers, bellying up to the bar and demanding whiskey, but the present spectacle was bound to run a close second.

It was like watching the old clown-car routine at the rodeo, only in reverse.

Instead of clowns streaming endlessly out of some run-down rig in the middle of a dusty arena, there were these beautiful women, all of them in impossibly full skirts, trying to squeeze a beleaguered bride into the front passenger seat.

The enterprise took at least five minutes of stuffing volumes of fabric inside, and Liam enjoyed every comical moment.

He had the decency not to laugh out loud, but only just.

Once Madison was contained—somewhat—the blonde managed to get behind the wheel with a little less fuss, but still considerable effort, and watching the remaining trio wedge themselves into the back was like something out of a Monty Python movie.

Finally, Ms. Bettencourt and her retinue were inside, except for the parts of their colorful gowns filling the car and spilling out the open windows, and the blonde executed a wide U-turn, narrowly missing the empty stagecoach standing in front of the livery stable as she did so.

Thank God the horses hadn't been hitched up yet.

Liam watched the vehicle—most likely a rental, given its nondescript design—until it zipped beneath the archway at the end of the street and finally disappeared.

Then he went back inside the saloon.

Costumed barmaids and dance-hall girls were arriving, having entered through the back way, tying apron strings and adjusting feathery headpieces as they came.

"Wait till you hear about that wedding over there at the lodge, boss," chuckled Sylvia Red Bird, the piano player and sometime torch singer. "Craziest one yet."

Liam pretended to be clueless. "You were there?"

"No," Sylvia replied, grinning. She was eccentric,

to say the least, dressing herself in trousers, a pointy-collared shirt, a striped vest and a top hat for her shift at the Hard Luck. Sometimes, when she helped out in the gift shop across the street, next to the old-time photography place, she wore authentic medicine-woman garb, which she created with her own hands. "Didn't need to be there. It's all over town what happened. The ceremony went off without a hitch, according to Miranda, from over at Bailey's restaurant, but when it came time for the reception, all hell broke loose. The bride shoved the groom right into the wedding cake, and his mother tumbled after him!"

Liam hid a grin. "Is that so?"

"It's so," verified Molly Steel, who was paying her way through community college over in neighboring Silver Hills by dancing with, and for, saloon patrons. "I saw the videos. They're all over YouTube and Instagram and probably TikTok, too. I laughed till I thought I'd die."

"You better show me those videos," Sylvia told Molly, "soon as we go on break."

Slowly, the saloon filled, first with staff, then with customers. Several of these, it soon became apparent, had been guests at the thwarted wedding.

There were a lot of toasts, followed by laughter and

anecdotes told from just about every perspective: the young and the old and everybody in between. The caterers. Even the groomsmen, who were all in a jocular mood, despite the groom—ostensibly their buddy—being dumped at his own wedding reception. They were knocking back liquor like there was no tomorrow, laughing a lot, shaking their heads at their friend Jeffrey's unnatural attachment to his mother.

Sheriff Eli Garrett showed up at eight o'clock or so, as he always did whenever there was a big shindig in or around Painted Pony Creek, accompanied by his good friend the chief of police, Melba Summers.

"Quite a day," Eli sighed, taking a place at the end of the bar.

"So I hear," Liam acknowledged. "Whiskey? Maybe a gin and tonic?"

Eli sighed. "I wish," he said. "I'm still on duty, so it's coffee for me, I'm afraid."

Melba, truly beautiful and tough as logging chain, stood beside Eli, smiling. "Sheriff's just trying to preserve his stellar reputation," she remarked. "Afraid I'll muscle in one of these election years and push him out of office."

Liam laughed, and so did Eli.

Both officers were served coffee—like always.

"The groom's mother, Yolanda somebody, turned up at my office a few hours ago, still coated in cake and frosting," Melba said. "She wanted the bride arrested for assault."

Eli nearly spit out his coffee. *"Assault?"*

"Well," Melba reminded him, "she *did* cause Mr. Sterne to topple backward into that mess. Do you have any idea what a cake like that *costs*, Eli Garrett?"

Eli sighed again, shoved a hand through his light brown hair. "Actually, Chief, I do. My wife orchestrates most of these events and it's downright scary the price of goods and services these days. It's not uncommon for the bridal gown alone to run in the thousands. And all for *one day*. I sure hope the star of *this* show got her money's worth, given the way the event turned out."

Melba sipped her coffee. "The bride," she said, "is a Bettencourt. You know, *those* Bettencourts, the ones who struck silver back in the day? The ones who built that big old house out at the end of Sparrow Bend Road? She's not hurting for money, I can tell you."

"I thought all the Bettencourts had died off, except for Coralee, of course," Eli said, in due time, having finished his coffee and shoved the cup away with a hint of reluctance. "And she's holding on by a thread, from what I've heard."

"Nope," Melba said, sounding pleased to set the sheriff straight on the matter. "She's got a granddaughter, Madison. The woman who was supposed to get married today. In my opinion, she came to her senses just in time to avoid tying herself down to a total waste of human bone and muscle."

Eli shook his head. "Small towns," he muttered. Then he thanked Liam and turned to leave.

At the Hard Luck Saloon, officers of the law got their sandwiches, sodas and coffee free. So did firefighters, paramedics and half a dozen old-timers who knew how to spin a damn good yarn.

From the sound of things, Madison Bettencourt was going to be starring in more than her fair share of tall tales for a long time to come.

And Liam wanted to hear every last one of them.

*Don't miss Madison and Liam's story,
available spring 2024!*